A SWEETWATER CHRISTMAS

ANNE HAGAN

Anne Hagan

To LJ for her persistence.

PUBLISHED BY:
Jug Run Press, USA

https://annehaganauthor.com/

CHAPTER 1

Emmie Skimmed a finger down to the next name. "Jorge Perez?"

"Here. You the teacher?"

"Your professor? No. That's Professor Fox. He'll be in, in just a couple of minutes. I'm his teaching assistant for the semester."

"Too bad," the man answered from his seat in the center of the classroom.

The man next to him elbowed him and said in a stage whisper, "Yeah because she's the fox."

Self-consciously, Emmie pushed a lock of hair behind her left ear then nudged the glasses she wore when she was in the classroom up just a little on her nose before continuing with the roll call. "Cassandra Prater?"

"Cass."

"Pardon?" She looked up from the list on the lectern and scanned the group of twenty or so mostly male students.

"I go by Cass," a woman at the far end of the front row, opposite of the door, responded.

Emmie looked at the short haired brunette perhaps a few moments longer than she should have. Cass stared right back. As she dropped her head back to her paperwork, she muttered, "I'll make a note." To herself she thought, *'They're not acting any better than my fourth graders do.'*

Just as she finished up the roll, Lucius Fox entered the room. "Ms. Warren." He smiled and dipped his head toward her in thanks.

She moved toward the back of the classroom and took her seat at the desk she'd reserved for herself before the students began filing in. As she opened her laptop and prepared to take notes, both for herself and for Lucius Fox, she couldn't help but glance to her left, across the room, at the brunette in the front row.

Lucius, having arranged his notes where the attendance paperwork had lain only moments before, clapped his hands together and rubbed them rapidly. "Let's get started ladies and gentlemen. I'm Dr. Lucius Fox. Welcome to Wind Energy 110, your introduction to wind power, and, by that, I don't mean what is being produced by what you had for supper tonight."

Laughter arose from the adults assembled in the room.

"First time in a college classroom for how many of you?"

Several hands in the room went up; Emmie guessed at least 15. She noticed Cass didn't raise hers. Shaking her head out and willing herself to focus, she made a quick note of the informal count for herself.

"Those of you that are first timers can see now that you're not alone in this. Just a couple of things about how we do things here, though. First of all, you can call me Dr. Fox, or Professor or you can call me Lucius; whatever you're most comfortable with. A little about me: I have a Ph.D. in education and a master's Degree in Electrical Engineering. I've been working at the wind farm as the chief engineer and Director of Operations for about ten years now. I spend part of my day, three days a week, right here in this classroom and in the turbine lab teaching the younger generation the same things you're going to be learning in the evenings over the next 18 months or so if you stick it out in this program we've set up for adult learners."

Emmie looked around with curiosity as a grumble started low in the classroom and rose.

Fox waved his hands to quiet the room. "I know what you're thinking," he said. "You're all competing for the same jobs, you and those teenagers just out of high school. About that, I want you to remember two things: One, where there's wind, there's work." He paused and let that sink in for a minute.

Emmie jotted that down in her own notes.

"Write that down," he said, seemingly reading her mind. "Stamp it on your forehead; do whatever it takes for you to remember that. If you finish this program, you're going to leave here with an Associate Degree in wind energy and something else those young fellas...sorry ladies, but they're mostly fellas, don't have; work and life experience. That's the second thing I want you to remember. You have valuable experience behind you that they don't have."

Heads nodded around the room.

"Now then, there's one other thing. In those folders Ms. Warren gave you as you entered this classroom this evening, there's a release form." He held an arm out toward her.

Emmie sat up a little straighter as most of the people in the classroom turned to look where he'd pointed.

"She's helping out the next couple of semesters as part of her research toward her master's thesis. She's going to be collecting a little data as we go along about each of you. Not your names or anything personally identifying; just some background information, fields you've worked in, that sort of thing. To be included in her research, you'll need to sign the release. That will go on file here with the college, not with her. Go ahead and do that now and pass them back to her. If you don't want to participate in any of her data collection efforts, please hang onto your form and speak with her privately, after class."

"She can collect all the data she wants from me," the man next to Jorge called out.

Uneasy laughter rose from a few people in the room and Lucius frowned but he didn't say anything.

Emmie stood and collected the forms as they drifted back to her. She received 22 in all.

She'd counted 23 students in the room. Someone didn't sign. She thought she knew who hadn't, but she didn't dare look through them. Besides, Fox was off and running.

Two hours later, as the new wind energy students filed out of the room, talking nervously about the first homework many of them had, had in years, Lucius Fox made his way back to Emmie.

"What'd you think?" he asked.

"You're already over my head with the technical stuff."

"No," he said dismissively as he shook his head. "You're brighter than that. You'll understand a lot more of it as we go along than you think you will."

"I didn't even buy the book, Professor."

"Lucius, please. Call me Lucius. We're going to be working together for a while Ms. Warren."

"Then," she smiled at him, "You'll have to call me Emmie."

"Only between us," he said, grinning back at her. "We don't need some of these um, men, to hear that and latch onto it."

Emmie nodded and then, with all the confidence she could muster, she said, "I was born and raised here in Texas. I can handle them."

Lucius looked around the nearly empty room. He noticed Cass lingering near her seat in the front. "Something I can help you with Miss?"

"Actually, I wanted a word with Ms. Warren."

"I see."

Lucius turned back to Emmie. "If you want to give me those

forms, I can run them by the administration office tomorrow morning when I'm back here. They're closed right now."

Emmie leaned toward him. "I think that's what she wants to talk about." She tipped her head slightly toward Cass. "I can drop them off Thursday evening when I get here, if that's all right?"

"I guess that's fine. Don't forget."

"I won't."

"Ladies," Lucius said, as he turned and stepped backwards to view them both. He tipped a couple of fingers to his head as he dipped it like he was doffing an imaginary cowboy hat.

Cass watched him leave before she approached. "Sorry to hold you up."

"No problem. How can I help you?"

"I think Professor Fox has taken quite a liking to you."

"Pardon?"

"Don't get offended. It's just something I noticed, is all. I notice things. That's my job."

"Then you've missed quite a lot. The Professor is married and I'm…I'm not in the market for dates, flings or anything else of that sort." *If she only knew,* Emmie thought.

"Whatever you say," Cass said. "I didn't come back here to argue with you."

"Why did you come back here?"

Cass held up the release form, face out. "This. I need just a little bit more information before I become someone's guinea pig."

Emmie did her best to control her temper as she addressed the brash woman. "It's not a requirement. You're free to skip participating and just go on your way whenever I'm…well, whenever I'm doing the things I need to do with the class for my research."

"Not very confident in yourself, are you, Emmie?" She said her name with added emphasis.

Emmie threw her hands up. "I thought you didn't want to

argue? Look, if that's all, I really do need to get going. I have a little bit of a drive to get home and I have work to do yet this evening."

"Abilene?" Cass asked, as Emmie gathered her things.

"Other direction. Other side of Sweetwater, here, out a little ways."

"Really?" Cass tilted her head and cocked an eyebrow.

Emmie glanced at her and then glanced quickly away. Rather than answer, she made a show of winding up the power cord for her laptop and stowing it in her bag.

"My nephew is a Junior on the team this year."

"That's nice for him. They're looking pretty good," she conceded as her tone went from sarcastic to monotone.

"You didn't even ask who he is," Cass pointed out.

"I'm sorry. Who, pray tell, is your nephew?" Emmie asked as she picked up the laptop bag and started for the door.

"Wow, you're something, you know? You'd catch more flies with just a little more honey, honey."

The strawberry blond whirled to face the other woman. "Don't call me honey!"

"Whoa! Sorry!" Cass held up her hands in mock surrender. She still had the release form in her left hand.

"Just give me that. I'll dispose of it on the way out."

"I'll walk out with you. Wouldn't do to have you walking out alone tonight."

"I can take care of myself."

"And I'm absolutely sure that you can but there's more safety in numbers and, besides, I didn't say I wasn't going to participate; only that I want more information."

Emmie sighed and started walking. Cass followed.

"What's the topic of your thesis?"

Emmie slowed and waited for the other woman to come alongside her. "How economic failure influences adult education."

"Ouch," Cass said.

"Is that a problem?"

"Not for me. I'm not an 'economic failure'."

"I never said you were. It's just that programs like this appeal to people trying to better themselves, get out of the cotton fields, off the ranch..."

"What's wrong with working on a ranch?"

Emmie groaned. It was coming out all wrong. "Nothing. I grew up on a ranch. It's practically the only life I've known."

"Obviously not; not if you're in a master's program. You've probably been a student most of your life...never had a real job."

"Now who's making assumptions?" Emmie flung back at Cass. She reached the door going out, pushed it open hard, then strode ahead toward her car. She wanted to put as much distance between herself and the insufferable Cassandra Prater as she could, as quickly as she could.

CHAPTER 2

"How was your class mommy?" six-year-old Seth Jr. asked her as he wandered into the room where she was grading math papers and insinuated himself in her lap.

"You're supposed to be in bed.," she scolded him. "You have school in the morning. We can't have Mrs. Stropich getting mad at me in the teacher's lounge tomorrow because you're asleep at your desk, now can we?"

"Lounge? What's that?"

"That's the place the teachers go to get away from all of you little hoodlums," his grandmother said as she entered the room.

"Sorry baby," she said to her daughter, "He got himself out of his bath and wandered down here on his own."

Trudy Oakes eyed the boy up and down. "At least you picked out matching pajamas and put them on this time. Now then, tell your mother goodnight and march on back upstairs young man. I'll be up to tuck you in, in just a minute. I need to talk to your mama for a second or two."

Seth gave Emmie a quick peck on the cheek, wished her a goodnight then did as he was told.

She called after the boy, "I love you bunches."

He stuck his face up to a gap between spindles in the stair railing and called back, "Love you bunches too mama!" then he scampered the rest of the way up.

"What's up?" she asked her mother when she was sure the boy was out of earshot.

"Nothing important, dear. I just wondered how it went, myself."

Emmie shrugged. "Fine, I guess. First night. Not much to tell."

"You're sure?"

Emmie squinted and looked at her mother. "Why, have you heard something different?"

Confusion clouded Trudy's face. "No. Should I have? You seem awfully wound up tonight…not your usual self."

"How on earth do you do that? You've only been in the room for two minutes!"

"A mother knows. One day, you'll see exactly what I mean."

Emmie thought of Seth and glanced toward the stairs. "There were a couple of things," she said, looking back at Trudy. "Nothing important. A typical Texas male, for one, acting like they do sometimes." She glanced back down at the math papers and twirled the red pencil she'd laid down on top of the stack when Seth showed up.

"What else?"

"Hmm?" She looked back up at her mother.

"You said there were a couple of things."

"Oh." She looked down at the papers again quickly and then back up. "There was just a woman in the class that didn't want to participate in my research, is all."

Trudy nodded then leaned back against the desk and studied her daughter. "About that," she said, after a time.

"What about it?"

"You'll be all done but the shooting match in what, about three or four months, right?"

"If the defense of my thesis of everything goes the way I expect with this last part? Yes."

"And then what?"

"And then I try to get a position teaching at a university in Abilene or Dallas or…Austin."

"Dallas? Austin?"

"Mom, we've talked about this. I don't want to teach fourth grade in Sweetwater forever."

"But what about Seth? He needs to grow up here, where his family is. He can't do that in Dallas or in Austin. Now, if you're in Abilene, he can…you can teach there and still live out here. What's so bad about that?"

Emmie, putting off for a moment answering a question she felt like she'd already answered a thousand times before, raised her hands to her head and rubbed her temples. "I know Mom, I know. I just…I just have to go where the opportunity is. What if there isn't anything for me in Abilene? It's not as big as Dallas or Austin." I just have to get away from here, she thought to herself. *I have to get to somewhere where I can finally be myself.*

"Think positive."

That's what I'm trying to do, Emmie thought.

"The good Lord will provide, child. He always provides."

And that's what I'm afraid of.

CHAPTER 3

Thursday Evening, September 8th

Emmie figured she'd be the first one in the classroom. She was mistaken. Cass was there waiting for her when she walked in.

The brunette stood by the desk Emmie had used the first night holding out a bright red apple in one hand and the signed release form in the other one.

"How long have you been standing there like that?"

"Well, hello to you too."

Emmie didn't respond. She put the laptop bag down on the chair and started unpacking it instead while Cass looked on, smiling.

Unable to bear the silence after more than a minute of it, Emmie broke it. "Did you get your homework done?"

"Of course, teach'. Wouldn't want to come to your class unprepared now, would I?"

"It's not my class."

"You're going for a Master's in education though, right?"

Emmie nodded.

"So, you're planning on teaching at the college level someday; am I right?"

"Yes, but not this."

"Let me guess; your BA is in English Lit?"

"No." Emmie gave Cass a tight-lipped grin.

"Not going to tell me, eh?"

"It isn't relevant."

"For me to know?"

"No. It's not relevant to my thesis. It was in early childhood education." Her tone was brusque.

Cass shook her head. "Look, I'm trying to extend an olive branch here. We got off on the wrong foot the other day. I don't have a problem with your research. I…I was just curious, is all. I brought these for you." She held out the apple and the form again.

Emmie paused for a beat and then accepted the form. "Thanks," she told her, "but you can keep the apple."

"Suit yourself," Cass said.

Emmie stared as the brunette polished it against her chest and then raised it for a bite and caught her looking. Embarrassed, she turned quickly away and busied herself with her computer.

Cass grinned broadly, turned and moved just a couple of desks down in the back row. She sat down, pulled out her text book and acted as though she hadn't noticed a thing, but she watched Emmie out of the corner of her eye as she munched on the apple and pretended to read.

Emmie tried to look anywhere but at Cass.

"Okay folks," Lucius said to the class, "that's a wrap for the first hour tonight. Take about a ten-minute break and then gather up in the hallway. I know you toured the turbine lab when you applied, but we're going to have it to ourselves tonight and I'd like to take you over there and show you a few things you have to look forward to once we get some of the theory out of the way."

Emmie stood and stretched as people started filing out of the room. She planned to give them a few minutes to use the restroom or take a smoke break and then she hoped to talk with a few of them informally in the hallway. She hazarded a glance to her left. Cass hadn't budged.

Lucius made his way back to them. Addressing Cass first, he asked, "Don't you want a break before we go over there?"

"Naw. I'm good, Lucius," she half shrugged.

"Suit yourself but there's no easy exit to the restroom once we start looking into the clean room."

Cass just nodded his way. Emmie picked her own brain during the exchange, trying to recall the clean room from her personal tour of the facility with the department chair just days before.

"There's a clean room for the turbine lab?" she asked Fox when she just couldn't picture it.

"Uh, yeah. Well, sort of. They share one with the sciences for testing lubrication mixtures and, uh, that sort of thing."

Emmie wasn't convinced that, that was the case at all, but she didn't feel right questioning Fox.

"Will you be going over with us…Ms. Warren?" Lucius asked her before she could frame any sort of a response at all.

"No, I don't think so. I've seen it. A tour isn't a good time for me to be poking around for answers to my questions. I'm sure they're going to have plenty of questions for you. I'll probably just head on home. I have…" she glanced sideways at Cass, "some things I need to take care of for tomorrow."

"Oh. Okay then. I guess," he glanced at Cass too, "I guess this is it. I'll see you back here Tuesday, right?"

She nodded. "Tuesday."

Once Lucius left the classroom, Cass rose. "I don't care what you say. That man has a thing for you, baby girl. Too bad he's clueless." She headed toward the door.

"Excuse me?"

She stopped, and half turned. "I said clueless."

"I heard what you said. What did you mean by it?"

"You know exactly what I meant." With that, she left too.

CHAPTER 4

Friday Evening, September 9th
Sweetwater Mustang Bowl

"Finally; halftime," Emmie groaned to her sister, her oldest sibling. She stood up from her seat in the ancient wooden bleachers and shook out her left leg. "I think it's asleep."

Her sister Cora leaned back and stretched her arms over her head. "It has been a real slow game, hasn't it?"

"Lord, you aren't kidding! Lowest scoring home opener I can remember." Emmie rubbed the back of her thigh and watched the long line of fans snaking out of the lower stands toward the concession stand and the bathrooms. "Why do we always have to sit way up here, anyway? I could really go for a Coke, but that line is going to take forever."

"So, we can have the rail to lean back on, silly and, besides, Tyler knows right where to find me in the crowd if he needs me."

"He's the quarterback. He's not down there lookin' for his mama!" Emmie chided Cora.

"Hey, you never know what's going to happen."

"Shush you! Don't even say such things! If our mama were here, she'd give you what for."

Cora ignored the warning. "If you really want a drink, you best be going. You might have a chance of making it through the line and back before kickoff. We start the second half with possession, remember?"

"I'm going, I'm going. I'll tell you this though, if that left guard doesn't start protecting a little better, you're going to have one banged up kid on your hands tonight."

Emmie joined the slow-moving line out of the stands, eventually reaching the track around the fenced in field. She shook her head in wonder as she looked down at the new cork running track. All this money on equipment and athletes, she thought, and none of it for the comfort of the fans.

"Hey Ms. Warren," a pre-teen boy called out from over to her right in the second row up in the last section of the stands.

She nodded her head and sketched a wave at her former student then laughed as his buddy next to him elbowed him.

"What are ya' hitting me for? She was my teacher in the third grade."

"I thought I recognized you. You're not wearing your glasses."

Emmie's head shot around to the left to find Cass walking along beside her.

"Where did you come from?"

"I told you; my nephew plays for the team. He sort of lives with me right now."

"Sort of? You live in Sweetwater?" Emmie was puzzled, and it showed in her tone.

"No, ah, Merkle. He's a transfer here. His parents, actually, just my sister, is in Abilene. When his dad left them a couple of years ago, he got a little hard for her to handle…got a case of the ass, I guess you'd say."

"Why isn't he playing in Merkle then?"

"Their team was set. They wouldn't take a walk on."

"Oh." Emmie continued on her way, not sure what else to say.

Cass kept close to her as they wound through the milling crowd. "Headed to the restroom?" she asked.

"Concession stand."

"Me too."

'Just great,' Emmie thought.

She reached the nearest stand about a half a step ahead of Cass. Taking her chances, she quickly chose a line and hoped it moved fast. She didn't want to miss the second half kickoff. The other woman fell in behind her.

"So, you're a teacher?"

"Yes," she answered without turning. She scanned the menu board instead wondering what Cora might want since she'd forgotten to ask.

"Third grade, I take it?"

"Fourth grade for the last couple of years."

"How long have you been teaching…if you don't mind my asking? I mean, you're the one that ought to be asking me questions, I guess, but…anyway."

Emmie half turned toward Cass then, resigned to playing twenty questions with the brash and nosy woman while they waited. "I'm off the clock right now, in both cases. To answer your question, this is my eighth year."

"Wow, you're kidding. I never would have guessed that. You look so…so young."

Emmie felt a blush creeping up her cheeks. She quickly turned to face the stand again and moved up a little as the line shifted. She drew in a breath and let it out slow and then another.

A man left the front of the line with a box carrier holding four drinks and a large bag of popcorn. The lines were tight, and he had to fight his way through. As he jostled along past them, Cass, trying to get out of his way, bumped into Emmie.

"Sorry. Sorry," she said as she latched onto an arm when she reached out to steady her.

Emmie was wearing a simple long sleeve hoodie in the relative warmth of the late summer evening. The other woman's touch was like an electric shock running through her. She jumped, not from being jostled, but from the surprise of her own reaction.

"Oops," Cass said. "I've got you all off kilter."

If she only knew, Emmie thought. She shook her head to clear it. "I'm fine. Fine. Almost lost my balance is all."

When Cass let go, Emmie instantly missed her touch.

"Hey Prater!" a guy addressed Cass from the line to their left.

She looked over at him. Recognition dawned in her eyes. "Lev."

"That nephew of yours better settle down in there. He's going to get our QB nailed if he doesn't step up."

Emmie eyed Cass. "The left guard is your nephew?"

"Jimmy Rogan, yep."

Cass switched right back to the man giving her a hard time. "He'll be just fine Lev. You wait. He's just getting started."

"I sure hope you're right."

"Me too," Emmie told her. "Tyler Haines, the Quarterback, is my nephew."

"What are the odds?" Cass muttered.

IT WAS TWENTY-ONE TO SEVENTEEN, Sweetwater down, with a minute and five seconds left to play, when they received a kickoff in their own end zone to start their last series with the ball on the twenty.

The home crowd was on its feet but subdued after the opposition touchdown and extra point conversion for them to take the lead moments before.

"I'm so glad Mama and Daddy decided to sit this one out and keep Seth tonight," Emmie said. "Daddy would be spitting nails right about now."

"You know he is, Em. He's got it playing on the radio," Cora reminded her.

Emmie felt her sister tense next to her as Tyler and his teammates took the field. "I wish they'd let Fred put one of his defensive backs in at left tackle. Even his second stringers would give Ty better protection than Rogan has been tonight," Cora said about her husband, the defensive line coach for Sweetwater.

"You're forgetting," Emmie reminded her, "that it was Fred's defense that just gave up a touchdown."

Cora shot her sister a sideways look but then started cheering as Tyler fell back in the slot and spiraled a nice pass toward the opposite sideline, far enough for the first down. His receiver got out of bounds to stop the clock. "Way to go Tyler! Good job boys!" she screamed.

The stands all around them erupted in excitement. A minute and two seconds remained on the clock.

"Plenty of time," Emmie said.

Tyler took the snap again. He fell back two steps then two more. He looked to the right down the field. His first look receiver was covered. He looked left. Rogan held his man as Tyler scanned for an open receiver on his weak side. The crowd started screaming and then it seemed as if time stood still when the guard on the right lost his grip on his man as he slipped and fell.

The defensive lineman made quick work of getting over the fallen guard and hitting Tyler hard, sending him crashing to the turf. The whistle blew. The boy managed to hang onto the ball, but he lay there, writhing in pain as the crowd looked on in near silence.

Cora scrambled past Emmie and raced down, out of the stands. Emmie followed.

A uniformed cop stopped her at the fence to the field.

"That's my son!" she screamed over his shoulder.

"I can't let you on the field ma'am. Just calm down. The docs already out there with him."

Emmie took her sister's arm then watched as the boys on both teams took a knee. She could finally see Ty again, surround by his coaches as he lay there. He was moving his legs. That was a good sign, she thought. He's going to have to come out for a play, is all.

CHAPTER 5

Friday Evening, September 9th

The hospital waiting room was crowded. Half the team had left the game as soon as it was over and shown up to support Tyler, without bothering to go to the locker room and change out of their uniforms.

Emmie waited off in a corner by herself. Only Cora and Fred were allowed in with Ty while he was being evaluated.

Their mother was calling her every ten minutes, asking for an update. Emmie didn't have anything to tell her other than that they were waiting for the x-rays.

She couldn't sit any longer. She got up out of her chair and wandered down the hallway toward the vending machines. As she stood there staring but not really seeing the contents the double doors next to the vending room opened. Cass wandered through them from the main part of the hospital.

"What...what are you doing here?"

"The team is mostly here, I take it?"

Emmie nodded.

"Jimmy wanted to come but he, ah, he has a curfew he has to keep…judge's orders." She turned her head away but continued talking. "Anyway, I ran him home and then I came in his place."

"You didn't have to. Tyler's going to be fine. He's complaining that his side hurts. He got out of the ambulance and walked in here on his own. He seems to be coherent."

Cass let out a breath she'd been holding. "Well, that's a relief."

Emmie nodded but stopped when the doors from the ER, back in the other direction swung open. She looked toward them and then started moving quickly that way when Fred stepped out and looked around. Three quarters of the people in the room looked at him expectantly.

He looked for Emmie then dipped his head slightly to acknowledge he'd seen her. He cleared his throat and addressed the whole room. "Thanks, everyone for coming. Tyler really appreciates it. Unfortunately, you can't all go back there to see him. You can't because he's just got a couple of cracked ribs and a pretty nasty bruise that will be with him for a while. They're taping him up right now and then they'll be letting him out of here."

A cheer went up. When the boys settled down again, one asked, "Will he be able to play next week, coach?"

The head coach jumped in then. "One day at a time fellas'. One day at a time. He needs to heal."

"I'm so sorry Coach Haines," a uniformed player called out.

Emmie looked at Cass and whispered, "That's the right guard."

"Not your fault, son," Fred Haines told the boy.

"Yeah it is Coach. I didn't plant my feet right."

"Tell you what," Fred said to him, "How about you and Coach Leeds work that out between you? I'm not laying blame son. We've all lost our footing playing this game. We've all been banged up playing it too. Ty's going to be just fine...good as new in a couple of weeks or so."

The boys started picking up their gear and moving outside. Fred made his way over to Emmie.

"We, ah, have a little bit of a situation," he began.

"What's up?"

"I rode over here in the ambulance with Ty. My car's back at the field. He's going to have to lay flat in the back of Cora's car and she's going to have to drop me off over there to pick up mine. Can you call your dad to come down here and get you?

"Yeah, sure..." Emmie started to say.

Cass interrupted. "Don't do that. I can run you home."

"No, no. I couldn't put you out like that. You're going completely the opposite way."

"You're not putting me out and, besides, you can use the opportunity to play twenty questions with me."

At Fred's expression, Emmie explained, "Cass is Jimmy Rogan's, um, aunt. She's also in the wind energy program I'm auditing as part of my master's thesis research."

CHAPTER 6

"Where to?" Cass asked as she reversed her pickup out of the parking space.

Emmie sighed. "How familiar are you with the area?"

"I grew up in Abilene, but my Mom's family is all from the Merkel and the Trent area, so I've been in and around Sweetwater a whole lot."

"How about northwest of town, up 117?"

Cass shook her head. "Around the gypsum mine? I know how to get to it."

"That's a start, but we'll be going a little way past that." Emmie shook her head and looked at Cass. "I really feel bad about putting you out."

"You're not. Don't even give it another thought. It's good for me to get out of the house for something other than work and class and, besides, Jimmy will be home beating himself up over his mistakes tonight. Maybe by the time I get back, he'll be in bed, sleeping it off."

"Won't he be up, wondering about Tyler?"

"Ah, good point. Let me call the house real quick." The

brunette punched some buttons on the little screen set into her dashboard. Within seconds, Emmie could hear a phone ringing.

The voice of an older woman came through the radio speakers. "Hello?"

"Hi Grandma, it's Cass."

"How's that boy doing? Jim's driving me out of my tree here, what with all his pacing around and all. Hang on."

"Jim!" the old lady called out without muffling the phone or waiting for an answer to her question. "It's Cass!"

Back to Cass, speaking only a half decibel or so lower than she'd just called to the teenager, she said, "He's comin'."

"That's fine Grandma. I just wanted to let you know that I'm dropping someone off at home a little outside of Sweetwater before I head back there. I don't want you thinking you have to wait up for me. You need your rest."

"I'll probably head on to bed then…once I know about that boy. You never said how he was."

"I'm here; I'm here too," Jimmy Rogan interrupted. "How's Ty? Is he okay?"

"He's fine, the both of you. He's got a couple of cracked ribs and some bad bruising. He's in some pain and he won't be able to play for a week or two but he's fine otherwise."

"Well, thank the good Lord for that!" the old lady said.

"Yes ma'am. Now both of you get on to bed. Jimmy, we got a lot to do in the morning."

It was the boy's turn to say, "Yes ma'am."

Emmie studied Cass as she punched the buttons to hang up the call and then made a couple of turns out of town.

Feeling the other woman's eyes on her, Cass asked, "What? What are you thinking about?"

"You said you're from Abilene tonight and, at the game, you told me Jimmy is too."

"Yeah?"

"So, you're living with your grandmother in Merkel, of all places?"

"Gran, my mother's mom, yeah. She had a bad fall about 18 months or so ago…couldn't manage around the house let alone everything else while she recovered."

"She's recovered now?"

Cass nodded.

"But you've stayed on?"

"Other things came up."

"Jimmy?"

"He's one of them, yes. I didn't want him running roughshod over her, for one."

Emmie grinned. "It sounds to me like your grandmother can handle him."

"Well, you got that right," Cass chuckled. "Still, he lacks direction a lot of the time. That's my main focus, to give him some. Never had any kids of my own, of course, but I always felt like my sister's kids were just as much mine, especially him."

"Sounds like you've helped raise them…or, at least, him."

"Yeah. It's tough out there, you know? Jobs are hard to find around here that pay half decent. My sister, Pam, she works her tail off and barely makes enough to get by but she's too prideful to take much help other than from me…me and Gram."

"Is that why you're in the wind energy program? So you can help out a little more?"

Cass shrugged and glanced over at Emmie. "Kind of; not directly."

Emmie was intrigued.

"This on the record?"

"That depends on what you have to say. Your name wouldn't be associated with it anyway."

"My mom's family are all Lute's."

"As in 'Lute Longhorns'?"

"Exactly."

Emmie turned her head toward the passenger side window, not sure how much to say.

"Grandpa died a few years ago."

"I remember," Emmie divulged. "My family all went to the funeral."

The other woman gave her a long look before turning back to concentrate on the road and continue with her story. Gran has kept most of the land, but she's sold off a lot of the longhorn cows other than about a dozen or so and a couple of the bulls. She just couldn't manage all of that, even with my help."

"Yours?"

"I've been one of her primary hands these last few years, but after Gramps' died, most of our other help drifted away. They didn't want to work for two women."

"I know how that goes…"

"Do you?"

Emmie's hackles rose. "Trust me; I do."

Cass shook her head and gestured with a hand. "Sorry. It's just frustrating sometimes."

Emmie just nodded.

"Grandma 's been talking to the State about turning most of the property into another wind farm. There's plenty of wind to go around, of course, but she wants to keep it on the down low for now. That's why I was so hesitant to work with you."

"So, you're doing this program as training, so you can run it?"

"More or less. I already have a degree in business that I worked more than seven years to get, nights and weekends."

"I wondered."

Cass gave her a quizzical look.

"You ah, didn't raise your hand when Lu…Professor Fox asked who had no previous college experience. Where'd you go?"

"Did some of it at McMurray in Abilene then, after I moved in full time with Gran, online with Tech while we were dealing with her hip. I just finished with them about six months ago."

Cass turned her truck onto Highway 117. "How far past the mines?"

"A few miles; we have about ten minutes or so…sorry."

"Quit saying that. It's fine."

Emmie didn't think it would be fine. She fell silent.

Cass left her to her thoughts for a minute or two but then got curious. "Will you tell me about you?"

She sighed. "There's not a whole lot to tell."

"I'm betting that's wrong." She smiled then, a big beautiful smile that lit up the cab of the truck. When Emmie didn't respond, she asked, "Where'd you go to school yourself?"

Emmie chuckled. "UT…in Austin."

"That's funny, why?"

"Because my family was crazy over it. They're…they're very Christian…let me put it that way. Mom wanted me to stay close, to go to Abilene Christian. Daddy convinced her to let me go to Austin." Her voice grew wistful.

"Let me guess; you didn't want to come home?"

The strawberry blond shook her head. "It's uh, it's different there, you know what I mean."

"Perfectly." Cass glanced at her passenger, then turned back to her driving and smiled a little to herself. "That where you figured it all out, then?" She waited. She didn't glance over at Emmie, just gave her a little space and a moment to gather her thoughts.

"I…I think so. I don't know…"

"You do know," Cass said firmly.

The response was several long seconds coming but it came. "Yes, I do know, but there's nothing I can do about it."

Cass shot her a look.

"It's too late to do anything…to…well it's too late now. Life got too complicated."

"How's that…" Cass started to ask. She didn't finish the question. A herd of longhorns was crossing the highway a couple of hundred yards ahead of them.

After braking hard and coming to a stop, she checked on her passenger. Emmie seemed none the worse for wear, but she stared straight ahead.

"Hey," Cass said softly. "Penny for them?"

Emmie shuddered. "I...I haven't thought about those times in years. I blocked it all out."

Cass half turned and leaned across the center console. "I can't make myself block out good times...better times."

Emmie turned toward her. "I didn't have a choice."

"I think you did," Cass said as she reached for the other woman. Looping one arm around her shoulders, she pulled her toward her in a warm embrace, their heads hugged together for a few moments. Cass placed her left hand on the side of Emmie's right leg and turned her just a bit more in the seat. She pulled back slightly, looked into the blonde's eyes and then dipped her head and touched her lips to Emmie's.

Her kiss was tender and sweet. Emmie felt herself drifting, wanting more. At first, she responded. It felt so good; a feeling she hadn't felt in years. But then, abruptly, she pulled back.

"We can't do this. I...I can't Cass. I'm so sorry..."

"No," Cass said, as she pulled away. "I'm the one who's sorry."

CHAPTER 7

Cass couldn't take the silence. She searched for something to say besides apologizing again.

Emmie was the one who broke their impasse. Clearing her throat, she told her, "You'll be turning right about a mile up ahead."

As she slowed, Cass knitted her brow, trying to recall what might be ahead besides long stretches of pasture land.

"Are you familiar with the Oakes' name?"

"What? I thought your name was Warren?"

"Mine is. I was married…it's, it's complicated." She rushed on before Cass could respond, "My family name is Oakes. You'll be turning onto our ranch."

"That explains a lot."

"It does?"

Cass answered a question with another question. "Just what are you planning on doing with your master's degree?"

Emmie sighed. "The plan was to go back to Austin and teach there or maybe go to Dallas or San Antonio."

"And now? Stuck at the ranch?"

"No. At least, not in the way you're thinking. It's…I've never really been very involved with that; not since chores when we were all growing up. I have brothers for that. I'll be stuck in Abilene though, probably."

"Abilene's not so bad."

Emmie half shrugged. "I guess. I was just looking for a little more...culture, let's say. A little more diversity."

All the diversity you want is right here under your nose, Cass thought. She slowed a little more when her headlights caught the gate entrance for the ranch. She made the turn onto the long, smooth dirt stretch bordered by wide swaths of grass and split rail fence.

"Ever been out here for anything?" Emmie asked.

"Uh, no. I'm sure it's something to see though in the daylight."

"Dad does take a lot of pride in it but it's still a cattle ranch."

Feeling a little self-conscience, Cass mentally checked herself and then shuddered. Dummy, she thought to herself, you won't even be getting out of the truck. You're just dropping her off. She hoped Emmie didn't see her distress.

As they crested a little rise, Cass caught site of the homestead and some of the nearby horse barns up ahead. There were lights on and a lot of commotion for a ranch at nearly 11:00 at night, she thought.

Thinking the same, Emmie spread her hands and shook her head as she asked out loud, "What now?"

Cass stopped just short of the house and both women jumped out.

Emmie rushed around to the front of the truck and scanned around. Cass stood quietly at her side taking in the scene in front of her.

A mare, spooked by something, had broken through a corral fence near one of the horse barns. An older man holding a coiled lariat and two younger men had formed a loose ring around her, but they were helpless to do anything while she bucked and stomped. She hadn't even noticed their arrival.

The older man tried to talk to the horse, but the mare wasn't having it. Whatever had spooked her she thought was still there and she was determined to stomp the life out of it.

Emmie looked at Cass. "Probably a rattler," she leaned close to her and whispered. "We had one in the barn over there last week, now this." Emmie pointed toward a second barn, a little further away. "Anyway, I should help." She moved away from the pickup, toward the horse, and took up a position about fifteen feet from her dad, between him and one of the other men.

Cass went the other way and did the same.

The horse either began to notice the presence of several humans around it or it just began to tire. Either way, the bucking and stomping slowed enough that the old man tried to approach her as he spoke to her in soothing tones. She danced away from him, closer to a man on the back side of their little ring.

The second man tried to move carefully toward her too but, still skittish, she lapped around the ring stopping at a point that put her out in front of Emmie, about 30 yards.

"We don't want to tighten up on her too much," the old man cautioned. "She's still scared." He weighed the bulk of the coil of rope in his left hand as he pulled the loop and a length of it into his right.

"You're sure you wanna try to rope her?" Cass asked him.

He turned toward her. "Plan too. She's mine. She might not spook if I move to throw. Might just let me do it."

The words were no sooner out of his mouth than the mare turned tail and lapped their circle twice, finally coming to rest about ten yards from Cass, facing across the ring at the third man. Cass knew it would be a bad throw angle for the old man but, if she had a rope, she thought she just might be able to collar the horse.

She sidestepped carefully toward the older cowboy she now figured was Emmie's father. She pointed at the rope and he handed it to her without a word.

Drifting carefully back to her right, she got a proper grip on the lariat, reared back and threw. The lasso sailed through the air, widened out over the mare's head and settled down around her neck.

Cass gave it a tug to pull it tight. The old man and the younger one on the other side both rushed toward her, assuming the horse would give her a fight. The mare did buck once and then again but then she settled down and looked at Cass. Cass cooed at her and approached her slowly.

The old man moved toward them both as Cass reached the horse and gave her a rub down her nose.

"Some mighty fine roping skills you have there, under pressure," he said, admiration in his voice and eyes as he patted his mare.

"Thanks," she said back. "I've had a lot of practice. Horses are a little easier than stray longhorns."

"That they are." He stuck out his hand, "Dusty Oakes."

"I'm Cass Prater," she told him as she shook his hand.

"Well thank you Cass." The old man took the rope from her and led the horse toward the second man who was still standing back a little in case the horse spooked again. He took the mare without a word and led it toward the barn. The third man followed.

Emmie moved over to Cass. "Thanks for your help...again. You've about filled your quota of good deeds for the day, haven't you?"

"How's Ty?" Dusty started to ask his daughter.

He was interrupted by Seth Jr. running out of the house, yelling, "Mommy, mommy!"

The boy ran headlong into Emmie and clung to her. "That horse went all crazy mommy. I was watching from the kitchen and..."

Emmie lifted the boy. "You're in your pajamas Seth. You shouldn't even be out here. In fact, you should be in bed," she scolded him. She whirled around holding him and headed toward the porch, forgetting all about Cass who was standing, temporarily shocked, at the little scene that had just played out before her.

"But mommy, she was making all that noise. She woke me up!" He didn't let up. "How'd that lady do that?" He asked as he pointed over Emmie's shoulder at Cass.

Emmie grabbed his hand. "It's not polite to point at people."

"Sorry," she said as she half turned back toward Cass. "His manners still need a lot of work."

The brunette waved Emmie off and smiled at the boy. "I've had lots of practice. Maybe when you're a little bigger, your grandpa could teach you."

The old man harrumphed. "I haven't got nearly the patience for that!"

"Well your Mommy here, then."

Dusty laughed and Emmie coughed. "That'd be the day," Dusty said.

"If you're all done making fun of me," Emmie told them, "I really do need to see that he gets back to bed." She resumed her march toward the porch.

Dusty looked at Cass. "I know it's late but the least we can do is offer you a beverage. Sweet tea? Coffee? We have some decaf, I think."

"Decaf sounds great."

The two of them followed Emmie and the boy inside. Emmie disappeared immediately with Seth making Cass wonder if she was overstepping again. She shrugged it off. She'd have a cup to humor the old man then hit the road.

CHAPTER 8

Emmie came back downstairs as Cass was draining the last of her cup.

"Sorry," she said looking from the other woman to her parents.

"It's okay sweetie," Trudy told her. "Cass filled us in on Ty while you handled Seth." She smiled at Cass. "Sometimes he's harder to corral than Tasha."

"Tasha?" Cass asked.

They all laughed but Cass. "That's the mare you roped," Emmie told her.

"Ah."

"Come on," Emmie said, "I'll walk you out."

Cass said her goodbyes to the Oakes' and followed the shorter woman out the screen door.

"Thanks for the ride and for your help," Emmie began.

"I see now where you get it."

"Get what?"

"Apologizing and thanking people constantly. It runs in the family."

"You should be thanked for what you've done, you know?" Emmie was a little indignant.

Cass dipped her head. "All in a day's work, ma'am."

They reached her truck, but she was in no hurry to climb in just then. "Your folks are good people."

Emmie nodded.

"They love you and that boy."

"Yes."

"Is…is his father in the picture?"

"He, uh, he died a little over a year ago, but he never really was in the picture."

"You were married."

"Yes; in name…to give Seth a name. His father died in an accident on an oil platform out in the Gulf. When he wasn't out there, he spent most of his time pub crawling his way around Galveston."

On hearing that, Cass couldn't help herself. "You know, there's plenty of Texas countryside out here to live in and let live. You could get a piece of land close enough to here to keep Seth's grandparents happy and to be free to be yourself."

"It's not that simple. I can't teach grade school, or middle school in Texas as a lesbian. I'd be lynched. I don't want to teach at that level forever anyway, but that's all there is for me here in Sweetwater."

"What about Abilene?"

"Sure, I could probably find something there and live my private life out here…until Seth's classmates find out that his mommy is gay. Kids are cruel! What then?"

"Okay, I get it. You're scared."

"You're damn right I'm scared."

Cass blew out a breath. "Now I should apologize. I shouldn't be pressing you. Hell, we barely know each other." *Even though I feel like I've known her all my life.*

She opened her door and climbed up into the cab but then she threw caution to the wind. "I'm going to live the way I want to, finally. There's a little ranch, just outside of Merkel that I'm buying. My offer for it was accepted this morning. I'll have my own, private little spread and I'll still be close enough to Gran to run the wind farm." Her eyes bored into Emmie's. "Maybe you could come out and visit some time..."

CHAPTER 9

Tuesday Evening, October 4th

Emmie walked into the administration office and made a beeline for the copier. She didn't often find it empty, and with only ten minutes until class, she expected a line of students to wait behind. She fed her survey forms into the machine, set the number of copies, then stood back to wait. She nodded at the student manning the desk but didn't bother with small talk.

A man's voice called out from one of the offices beyond the counter, "Cassandra Prater? I can see you now." He stepped out into the open and looked toward Emmie, but she didn't see his questioning glance. Her head shot around, looking for Cass.

The student spoke up, "She stepped out to take a call. I'll go and get..." Before he could finish his offer, the door opened, and Cass walked in.

Emmie tried not to look at the other woman as she willed the copier to finish the print job quickly.

"Cassandra, I presume?" the counselor asked.

"Cass. Just Cass."

Emmie grinned. She couldn't help herself.

He waved toward the opening at the end of the counter. "Let's go back to my office."

"I have class in a few minutes. I just need you to look into something for me," Cass said, as she stepped up to the counter instead. "I received a notice that I'm not enrolled for an English course this semester and that I also need to take some other core courses as my wind energy program progresses."

"Yes, that's correct," he said nodding. "But, I'm afraid you're already late enrolling for the English this semester. That's why we sent the notice. You're going to have to double up on common core next semester if you want to keep pace with your current class."

Emmie bristled but didn't turn. *Cass doesn't need those classes if she has the degree she says she does.*

"I already have a bachelor's degree. I don't need the core curriculum classes. My transcripts should be in your files."

"Hmm. That's odd."

Emmie gave up all pretenses of disinterest and watched as the student aide left the counter, went to a desk and leaned over a keyboard. Cass glanced at her but then focused right back on the much younger student.

"P - R - A - T - E -R, right?" He spelled out.

"Yes."

He shook his head as he looked back at her. "It doesn't show here. Did you give us a transcript?"

Cass blew out an exasperated breath. "With my initial application. On paper."

The younger man shrugged. "Should of been scanned in."

Cass looked back at the career counselor still standing there, offering nothing in the way of help. "Don't you people keep anything on paper?"

"No need to. Files just take up space. The database is all we have now." He held his hands up in mock surrender.

"So, I have to submit everything again?"

"If you've got it..." he started to say. His tone was skeptical.

Cass didn't miss the implication of his words. "I'm telling you, I have a full transcript and a diploma. I walked in the graduation ceremony. I've got the degree. You admitted me here based on transcripts I submitted. I can't help it that you don't have them in your little computer over there, but it doesn't mean I need to prove myself or take common core classes all over again, for Pete's sake. Just call admin at McMurray or at Texas Tech. They'll get my paperwork over here to you and get this all straightened out."

Emmie stepped up to the counter and touched Cass's forearm, drawing her ire away from the two men on the other side of the counter. "I know Sue Levitt in admissions at Texas Tech. I can call her and see if she can speed things up for you."

"Thanks for your help back there." Cass suppressed a shudder as she walked down the hallway, next to Emmie. "I was ready to strangle that guy...his smug look. He didn't believe a word I said."

Emmie glanced at Cass and then looked away. "I didn't want to say anything in there but...I've been auditing some of the classes that are a little further along in the program. They admit twenty to twenty-five new students here every semester. There's a lot of drop off when a group gets a couple or three semesters in. I didn't want to see you become one of their dumb statistics over a mix up in records."

"What do you mean, drop off? People quit?"

Emmie bobbed her head and then stepped through the classroom door, with Cass following right behind. "A lot of the older students - almost all of them men - get frustrated with the core classes and then they start to fall behind in the technical curriculum," she continued, her voice lower.

"Is that all part of your thesis research?"

Emmie answered with a tight-lipped nod.

Cass dipped her head toward the shorter woman. "I wouldn't want to be one of your statistics either." With that, she turned and sauntered toward her usual seat at the front of the room.

CHAPTER 10

Friday Evening, October 28th
Sweetwater Mustang Bowl

"Cass! Up here!" Dusty Oakes called to the tall cowgirl scanning the crowded stands for a vacant seat. "He waved an arm at her then sat back down next to his daughters when the brunette waved a hand back in acknowledgment and mounted the first step.

Emmie's eyes grew wide from her seat just off the end of the aisle, as Cass headed for them.

"You two move in a little," Dusty commanded from his own seat in the middle of the row, when Cass got close. Let the woman take a load off." He watched as Emmie and Cora did his bidding then smiled at Cass when she stopped alongside their position on the top row. "Have a seat there next to Emmie, if you like. How you been? Roped any more crazed mares lately?"

With a puzzled expression on her face, Cora looked back and

forth between her father and the woman now sitting beside her sister.

"No sir. Not lately," she replied as she smiled and sketched a wave at him. Turning her attention to Emmie, she said, "Hi there. Full house for the last game, eh?"

"I'll say," Emmie nodded.

Cora butted in, her curiosity spilling over, "You're Rogan's mother, right? I'm Cora, Ty's mother." She leaned out around Emmie and offered a hand to Cass.

Cass laughed. "Not hardly," she said as she shook Cora's hand. "Jimmy's my nephew. He stays with me though. His mama...my sister, is in Abilene. My niece fell ill, so they couldn't make it tonight."

"Sorry to hear that. The crud is going around, I guess. That's why my mom isn't here. She stayed home with Emmie's boy. He's got it." Cora jerked a finger at her sister then changed the subject. "Should be a good game, but the boys are playoff bound no matter what."

"Undefeated too, thank heaven. That was quite a scare for Ty last month. I was glad to see him come back, strong as ever."

"Sh! Don't jinx us," Cora said, as she put a finger to her lips.

Cass ignored Cora's superstitious barb. Instead she looked at Emmie and leaned back a little. "Sorry, Em'. I didn't mean to be rude."

Emmie raised an eyebrow at Cass calling her 'Em', something her family sometimes did but no one outside of the Oakes' name. She tried to play it cool and just shrug at the woman now sitting awfully close to her. So close, she could feel the heat of her all the way up her right side, from ankle to shoulder.

"Okay, so how does everyone already know each other here?" Cora asked. "First dad and now, 'Em', here." She looked at her sister and waited for an explanation.

"I, uh, met her over at the college," Emmie said. "She ran me home the night Ty got hurt. When we got to the ranch, Dad and the boys were trying to settle a mare that was kicking up a fuss and she, uh, she pitched in to help." Emmie mentally kicked herself for being thrown so off guard by Cass.

Seemingly satisfied with the answer and not noticing her sister's discomfort, Cora turned to her father and pointed down to the field. The team started to emerge from the locker room, led by Ty and his co-captain.

Cass bent her head to Emmie's ear to say something when the game announcer came over the loudspeaker and called the crowd to their feet to cheer on the team. Emmie didn't catch what she said, but the feel of Cass's breath in her ear had her shivering despite the warm evening air.

"THIS IS A REAL NAIL BITER," Cora offered to her sister at half time.

"Emmie looked at her hands and then at her sister. "Yeah...me too. Literally. We're only down by five though."

Cass stood. "I'm headed to the concession stand. This one's got me a little parched." She looked down at Emmie and asked, "Wanna come along?"

Emmie shook her head. "No thanks. I'm good."

"Cora? Dusty?" She held out a hand.

Dusty Oakes rose. "Might as well stretch the old legs, walk around and see what the scuttlebutt is."

Emmie let her father out of the row and then resumed her seat. She watched the retreating back of Cass until she stepped off the bottom riser and turned right toward the concessions area with Dusty right beside her.

"Earth to Emmie!" Cora called out. When Emmie half turned toward her, she gave her sister an odd look and asked, "Are you all right? You're awfully quiet tonight."

"Sorry. I...I'm fine. Just a lot on my mind, is all. I...Cass being here reminded me how much work I have to do on my thesis. I probably should have stayed home."

"And missed the last game?"

"They're going to the playoffs."

"That's not the point." Cora looked away for a second and let out a heavy breath. She turned back and picked up her sister's hand and waited until Emmie looked her in the eyes. "Is that all that's bothering you? I just…I sense there's something else going on. Anything you want to talk about?"

"Tight game, tight game, eh Cora?" Lou Hatton called from his seat two rows down, where he stood stretching his arms as he looked up at them.

Emmie breathed an internal sigh of relief when Cora dropped her hand and called back to Hatton.

* * *

"TOUGH LOSS LAST NIGHT," Emmie said to Cora, when she found her sister coming up the porch stairs from the driveway. "How are Ty and Fred taking it?"

"Not as bad as me, apparently. They're in the den watching college ball and talking about the playoffs during the commercials. I had to get out of there. Where you headed?"

"Right here." Emmie pointed to a rocker a couple of feet away. "It's hot in the house but there's a breeze out here."

"Mind if I join you?"

She waved a hand at the other chair. "Be my guest. Mom's in the back, picking the last remnants of the garden but I suspect she'll give up and be around soon. Seth is *helping*."

"Ugh!" Cora laughed. "Yeah, we know how that goes."

They sat in companionable silence for several minutes. Cora stole the occasional glance at Emmie who sat, eyes closed, rocking gently.

Emmie opened her eyes and looked at Cora. "What? I can feel your stare."

"I wasn't staring!"

"Cora, I've known you all my life. What's on your mind?" Emmie was sure she was going to pick up where they'd left off the night before. She closed her eyes again and suppressed a shudder.

"Look at me, please," Cora demanded.

Emmie opened her eyes and rolled them for full effect.

Her older sister wagged a finger at her. "Don't even start with me!" She paused and then jumped in, "What happened last night?"

"I told you what was going on. My thesis, remember? It's what I've been working on all day…until now, anyway."

"Yeah, yeah. I get that, but that's not it. You were fine until that woman…until Cass showed up. I picked up a lot of tension there."

Emmie shook her head no.

"Don't say no. I did. I know these things. I know you, just like you know me. What's going on? Have you had some sort of disagreement or something with her?"

Emily stopped rocking and gave her sister a long look. After taking a deep breath she began, "It's nothing like that. It's…it's comp…"

Trudy Oakes came around the corner of the house, to the porch with Seth in tow. "Take him in the house and dump him in the tub," she directed at Emmie. "He's been digging up grubs with his bare hands, *again*!"

CHAPTER 11

Early Saturday Afternoon, November 5th

Emmie twisted her key in the lock and opened the little door to peer inside. The box was stuffed with mail. She started pulling it out a couple of pieces at a time as she chided herself for not stopping to collect it more often.

She took the pile over to the writing table and began to sift through it. The catalogs she dropped straight into the trash bin. Most of the bulk mail followed those but she stopped cold and forgot all about getting rid of everything she considered junk when she found a letter in the remaining stack that was addressed to her from Texas Tech.

Hands shaking, expecting rejection, she tore an end off the long, thin envelope. After scanning the two pages enclosed, she stuffed them back into the envelope, put that in the pocket of her windbreaker and left, carrying everything else she'd collected and hadn't tossed away to her car.

Her decision was made even before she started the engine.

Rather than head northwest out of town, she worked her way south and east and onto the I-20 expressway. She passed through Trent and kept going. Just before she hit the city limits of Merkel, she jumped off the highway onto the frontage road, avoiding continuing onto the bypass around the sleepy little town. It had been a while since she'd bothered going into Merkel. It was faster to just go around it on the way to Abilene.

She remembered the address by heart, but she wasn't sure how to get there. A local florist was happy to provide a potted cactus and turn by turn instructions, getting her back on her way in less than five minutes.

At the pile of stone rubble she'd been advised to watch out for, she slowed and looked for the driveway. She found it fifty yards later. She sucked in a deep breath and let it out slow then shuddered a little wondering if she was being too presumptuous.

Fifty yards and a large measure of courage down a tree lined driveway later, she drove into an open area and stopped. Ahead on the right was an old but well-kept, two-story farmhouse. To her left, Jimmy Rogan stood working, not missing a beat with the post hole diggers he was using, as he watched her roll to a stop.

She leaned over to the passenger seat and picked up the cactus then patted her pocket to make sure the letter was still tucked away then she breathed in deep again and got out of the car.

"Ma'am," Rogan raised a hand almost to the brim of his hat as he acknowledged her presence.

She headed toward him. "Nice season Jimmy. You played hard. You all did."

He nodded but kept digging as he spoke. "Just hope we can keep it up through the playoffs, now. That first game's already gonna' be a tough one."

"I'm surprised the line coach hasn't got you in watching tape today."

"Actually, we're due in at 2:00. Was given' us a little break this morning for winning out last night, is how he put it."

Emmie chuckled. "You're not getting much of a break, digging post holes like that. You know they make a machine that does that right?"

"Yeah, about that…I, uh, broke it. It won't turn. That's why I'm doin' it this way."

"I see."

"If you're looking for Aunt Cass, she's off over there in the tool shed, trying to figure out what's wrong with it." He swung an arm behind him to his right but then went right back to his task.

"Good luck next week," Emmie told him as she started to walk away only to see Cass step out of the shed and come toward her carrying a gas-powered digger.

Emmie, still clutching the potted cactus, sketched a wave at her. Her stomach felt like it was tied in knots. 'Relax,' she told herself. 'You see her a couple of days a week…'

Cass smiled when she recognized Emmie. "What brings you all the way out here?"

"You did invite me out to see the place a…a while back."

She nodded. "That I did."

Veering toward Jimmy, Cass said to him, "You're probably getting hungry about now, aren't you?"

The teenager shrugged. "I could eat."

"Well, you can knock off on that." She pulled some money out of her pocket and held it out to him. "Drop this digger off at Nate's on your way into town. He's going to take a look at it. Then, get yourself a sub before you head over to the field house."

"Thanks." He took the money from her and put it in his shirt pocket then he took the post hole digger from her and reached for the manual ones he'd been using.

"Leave those. I'll put them away. You need to get going or you'll be late."

"Okay…sorry about this." He held up the piece of machinery in his hand like it weighed next to nothing.

"You don't need to be sorry unless Nate can't fix it."

The two women watched as Jimmy put the digger in the bed of an old Ford and then got in, turned it and drove away.

"That for me?" Cass pointed at the cactus.

Emmie held it out "A uh, a little housewarming gift, I guess you could say."

"A prickly cactus, huh? Just what are you trying to say?"

Emmie looked stricken.

Cass took it from her, laughing. "I was just teasing. Come on; let me show you around."

Emmie followed half a step behind Cass as she led her toward one of the two small barns nearby.

"This is my pride and joy. We've spent the past month, him and I and my sister when she has the time, converting this into a proper stable. I moved my horses up here over the past couple of days. We're putting in the fence posts for a paddock and then it'll be all done. It's not very big, now, but it's just right for me."

Emmie looked all around, taking it all in. "Cass, I love it. It's just as functional as our big horse barn out at the ranch is and, you're probably right, just what you need for a spread this size."

"I have 80 acres. Not enough to farm commercially but enough to feed…well, me, Gram and Jimmy and to play on and do what I want to do when I want to do it."

"Can't argue with that."

They fell silent as they left the stable and headed toward the other, slightly larger barn. Cass broke the awkward quiet between them. "How's Seth?"

"Good. He's doing good. He's out for the day with my sister and her family. I needed to do a little work on my thesis this morning."

"How's that coming?"

"I'm almost finished. In fact, I'll be submitting it within the next two weeks. My final exams for my last two classes are just before the Christmas break. I'll have to wait until the middle of January to defend it, probably."

"Will you have to go to Austin for that?"

"Yeah," Emmie nodded. "One last time."

Cass stopped and turned to face her. "You're not going down there and staying?"

"No; I'm not staying in Austin."

"Good." Cass turned quickly back away and started to walk into the other barn.

Emmie swallowed hard and put a hand on her arm, stopping her. She took the letter out of her jacket pocket and, wordlessly handed it to Cass.

"What's this?"

"Read it," Emmie told the other woman as she took the cactus from her and held it.

Cass pinched the sides of the envelope and slid the folded sheets out. She unfolded them carefully and started reading. Seconds later she shook her head and looked at Emmie. "You're going to be teaching at Texas Tech? Right here? Right at the branch campus in Abilene, I mean?"

Emmie smiled with relief and nodded. "In the fall. I'll finish out the school year at Sweetwater. All of that is dependent on a successful defense of my thesis, of course."

Cass read a little more. "In the mathematics department?"

Emmie nodded again. "It's mostly pharmacy and medical students over there but, yeah, they have to have their math prerequisites too. It gets me started. I'll just be a junior professor."

"Just?" Cass shook her head. "And, I guess I don't get it. What does your thesis have to do with teaching math?"

"Uh, only everything!"

"I don't know what to say…congratulations?"

Emmie set the cactus on the ground, took a deep breath and exhaled slowly then she fixed her gaze on Cass. "That's a start but I think you can do better." She moved up next to the other woman facing her and looped her arms around her waist.

"Yes ma'am," Cass said. She dipped her head and, without hesitation, touched her lips to the blonde's as she pulled her into a tight embrace.

Emmie felt like time stood still as she lost herself in Cass's kiss and her touch. Her senses were reeling.

They stayed that way for several minutes, but as the other woman's hands began to roam, stroking Emmie's back and sides and cupping her behind, Emmie drug her lips away and looked Cass in the eye.

"I think we need to finish the tour," she said, her breath ragged.

"Now? Uh...whoo...okay." Cass let out a heavy breath and tried to collect herself.

"Let's move on to the house; start with the bedroom. Your bedroom."

Cass looked surprised. "You're sure?"

"It's been so long...way too long."

CHAPTER 12

Cass leaned into Emmie, gathered her close and kissed her again as she walked her backwards toward her bed.

When the backs of Emmie's knees touched the edge of the bed, she leaned back into it and pulled Cass along with her. The weight of the other woman, pressed against her, had her groaning in pleasure, her body tingling.

Cass swiped her tongue through Emmie's mouth, tasting her. Emmie moaned underneath her and ran her hands up and down her back.

When Cass pulled back, she smiled at the blush of desire coloring Emmie's face and neck. "Still sure?"

"I'm absolutely sure!"

Cass lifted Emmie's hair away from her neck and kissed along the contour of her shoulder. She leaned up over the other woman and kissed her mouth, gently, at the corner. Emmie turned her head back to the taller woman behind her and offered her lips. Cass took them and kissed her deeply this time.

Emmie moaned. The kiss was heat and passion and so much

more. She tried to shift in the stronger woman's embrace to bring them side by side, face to face.

Cass had other ideas. She eased back down, on her back, her head now propped on her pillows then eased Emmie in front of her, leaning back into her. She began to caress and stroke every bit of Emmie's skin she could reach.

As Cass touched her, Emmie could feel the heat of her body and melted into her. Cass slipped a hand between her legs and stroked her curls.

Her touch was electric. Emmie spread her legs and dropped one knee over Cass's leg as she tried to guide her hand lower.

She began to move her fingers along Emmie's slit. Her other hand found her breasts and she kneaded the flesh, rubbing tiny circles over her nipples.

Emmie moaned and arched at the hips. When she did, she could feel the hard tips of Cass's nipples brushing against her back and shoulders as she writhed atop her.

Cass teased Emmie's clit gently at first but grew bolder with each husky breath the other woman took. She stroked along her slit, spreading her moisture up and around her clit with loving caresses. Then, dipping a fingertip between the folds, she pushed up and in.

Emmie ground back into Cass and squirmed when she felt the heat of the other woman's own desire against her backside.

Cass worked the finger further inside and then added a second.

Emmie bucked and begged for more, for her to move faster and deeper, but Cass worked at her own, slow, tortuous pace. "We have a lifetime," she told her.

LATER, as they lay curled up together in a tangle of sheets, Cass's fingers drawing lazy circles on one of Emmie's breasts, Emmie propped herself up on an elbow and looked down at her lover. "I love you Cass Prater."

"And I love you. I have since we first tangled over that stupid release form."

Emmie leaned in for a quick kiss then leaned back again. "So, does your offer…at least the one you implied that night out at the ranch, does that still stand?"

"Anything I've ever said you could have is yours."

"So then, when can we move in?"

"We?"

"Well, me and Seth, of course."

"Of course."

CHAPTER 13

Sunday Morning, November 6th

Emmie sat in the pew quietly, her appearance giving no indication of the turmoil in her head.

Her mother nudged her and whispered, "The sign of peace."

At peace she wasn't, but she shook her head to clear it and smiled at her mother as she took her hand.

"Where's your head at today, child?" Trudy asked.

Emmie didn't answer. Instead, she turned to old Mrs. Frankle on her right and offered a smile and her hand to her. *This will probably be the last time I'm ever allowed to set foot in this church.*

She figured the time after Sunday dinner was as good a time as any to broach the subject of moving away; moving in with Cass, to her parents. Cora would be there. She smiled at her sister in the pew behind them.

Cora ignored Emmie's offered hand and pulled her sister into a hug instead. *Maybe she'll be on my side,* Emmie thought.

She turned back to the front as the pastor began to speak

again but she didn't really hear him. Her thoughts turned again to Seth. She'd spent a sleepless night wondering what to tell her son. She still didn't have any answers.

* * *

"Regardless of all the rest, and I don't even know where to begin with that," Trudy Oakes was lecturing, her finger shaking at Emmie, "there's Seth to think about. Why, you can't just pick up and move him. You can't. He's already had enough instability in his young life without his father being present and there for him, even when he was alive. He won't want to leave his school, leave his friends."

"Mother, he's only six!"

"Maybe so, but he was telling me in the garden, just yesterday, how he wants to have you as a teacher in fourth grade. He only has two years to go, after all. Surely, you could hold out for at least that long?"

And then what? Another couple of years until he's out of middle school? Emmie took a deep breath. "That's the other thing. This will be my last year at Sweetwater. I'll be teaching math classes at the Texas Tech branch campus in Abilene starting next fall… provided my master's is complete." Emmie glanced around the table. Her father's face was expressionless. Fred sat playing with his fork. Ty looked uncomfortable. Cora, meanwhile, was silent, taking everything in. Emmie locked eyes with her for a split second before focusing back on their mother.

Trudy wasn't done. She tried to call in reinforcements. "Dusty, say something! Do something!"

"I…I…" He spread his hands and shook his head, helpless. "I don't know what to say." He looked down the table at his wife. "What do you want me to say? You knew she didn't plan on teaching there forever."

"That's all you've taken out of all of this?" Trudy threw up her own hands and gave him a hard look. He shrugged and turned his face away from her gaze.

"I'll tell you what, I'm dead set against you moving anywhere, especially if that means taking Seth along with you. That boy belongs in Sweetwater, around his family on the ranch where he's grown up. Not in Merkel where he has no one. This is his home."

Emmie caught a slight nod from her father, out of the corner of her eye. He was leaning toward his wife. "He'll have me. I am his mother and we won't be that far away. Merkle isn't at the other end of the earth for God's sake."

"Watch your mouth, young lady!" Trudy said, half rising from her chair. "You will not take the Lord's name in vain in this house. You know better."

"Mom," Cora said, "She just meant…"

The finger turned on the older daughter. "Meant what? Don't tell me you support this?"

Fred stood, tapped Ty's shoulder and motioned for him to leave the table with him. "Let's go see what Seth's up to."

Cora shot her husband a look but didn't try to keep him there. Instead, she responded to her mother's question with one of her own. "Don't you think Emmie deserves to be happy? To follow her own life?"

Dusty found his voice. "You can do what you want. You're a grown woman. We can't make you stay here, but you need to think of the boy. Like your mother, I'm worried about seeing my grandson and I'm also worried about what kids might do to him when word gets around about what's really going on. She's a good woman, Cass is, but come on Em! Kids can be so cruel."

So can parents.

Trudy leaned back in her chair, arms folded. She was quiet for a long time. No one moved until she spoke again. "How about this? How about you go ahead and move? Try your little experiment with this woman," she said, flipping a hand in the air.

Emmie started to interrupt, but Trudy cautioned her, "Wait. Let me finish. Move. Try this out but leave Seth here. Leave him out of it until you're sure this is what you really want."

"Mom," Cora stepped in again, "Mom, I love you, but I'm telling you; back off. You can't dictate to her." She flung a hand in Emmie's direction. "You can't dictate to any of us."

Trudy turned her ire on her eldest daughter. "Think about what you're saying! I'm trying to protect her. I'm trying to protect my grandson! What will people think?"

Cora shot back, "What will people think, or what will people think about you? This is really all about your image, isn't it?"

"That's enough," Dusty said, as he rose. "I won't have you speaking to your mother like that." He looked at both of his daughters. "I don't pretend to understand this, but you're right. Emmie, you're a grown woman. If this is what you want, so be it. Just be very careful what you do and how you do it. The only one who's going to be hurt here is that boy. I won't have that."

Trudy sighed. There was no point arguing any further once Dusty said his piece. Instead, she asked, "When are you planning to move?"

"Over the Christmas break, I think. I'll start my new position, in Abilene after the summer break but there's my thesis defense in January and then lots that needs to be done at...at Cass's new ranch over the summer. Moving in the spring or summer will be a lot more difficult."

"What about Seth, Em?" her father asked. "What about the rest of his school year? Why not leave him here to finish out for now?"

"Dad, I'll be finishing out the year at Sweetwater myself. I can bring Seth back and forth with me, just like I do now."

Trudy Oakes sighed. "Please, at least consider having him stay here for the rest of the school year. This is his home right now. One adjustment at a time, please?"

Emmie didn't see the advantage of having him have to adjust

to her not being there and then to moving him later, but she knew when to give up the fight. “Fine. Seth stays here until the end of the school year.”

CHAPTER 14

Monday Afternoon, November 7th

Emmie looked down at the paper in front of her and sighed. She'd gone over the ten long division problems on it three times without really seeing it.

A shadow passed across her desk. She looked up. Seth was still sitting at a desk in the front row, doing his own assignment. She turned and looked to her left. Cora stood in her classroom doorway.

As her sister came forward, she asked, "Not in any rush to get home, I take it?"

Emmie braced her hands against the edge of her desk. "This isn't really the time." She tipped her head toward Seth.

Cora nodded. "I'm sure the walls have ears too."

"You didn't come all the way over here to see me, did you?"

"No. There's a booster's meeting at the high school. I'm running a little early. Saw your car, so I swung in. Do you have class tonight?"

"No."

"Can we talk later then?"

"You're sure you want to be seen associating with me?"

"Come on little sister; it's not that bad. Take Seth and go on home. I'll pick you up around six o'clock."

"Maybe I better just meet you somewhere. We don't need Mom coming down on you any more than she already has."

"I HAVE TO SAY, you surprised me yesterday."

Cora put down her soda and smiled. "Can I say something to you that you promise not to take offense to?"

"What?"

"I figured it out when you were in college. Now, that's not to say your marriage to Seth Sr. Didn't throw me for a loop. It did. But, when he died, I kind of figured you might come back around to the real you."

"It doesn't upset you?"

"You're my sister and I love you."

"Not even a little bit?"

"Oh, I admit, it was hard to accept at first but all I ever wanted for you, for myself, for anybody, really, is for them to be happy. That girl, back then, obviously made you happy."

Emmie furrowed her brow. "What girl? Who are we talking about?" She couldn't recall her sister ever meeting any of the few women she'd dated while she was in college.

"Kelly? The girl you had come up for fair week the summer after your freshman year?"

"Kelly and I weren't...we weren't...She was just my roommate. We were friends. That's all."

"You're denying you had feelings for her?"

Emmie looked away.

"Em, it was so obvious. You two were so into each other. You only had eyes for each other."

"No," Emmie said, as she looked back at her sister, the blush still staining her cheeks. She put her hands up to them self-consciously. *I'm getting too old for this.* "She didn't feel that way about me. We never...I suffered that in silence. I…I was just starting to realize."

"Whatever you say," Cora said. "I could see it. Maybe she couldn't admit it to herself back then either, but the attraction was mutual. Besides, that's not the only time. She wasn't the first. She's just the one who got me to come to terms with it."

Emmie raised both hands in protest. "There wasn't anyone before that; I swear!"

"Really? There wasn't?"

Emmie shook her head vigorously.

"High school? My best friend Bonnie Hall? You mooned around after her like a lovesick puppy. I just didn't know enough to see it then. It all made sense after I saw the way you and Kelly were with each other."

Emmie coughed on her own soda then patted her chest hard, to clear the burn. She changed the subject. "Do you think Mama and Daddy will ever come around?"

"Mom's in shock, Em. She may get there, she may not, but it won't be soon. Can I ask, what have you said to Seth? Does he know yet?"

"Nothing…not yet." She sighed. "I suppose I'll have to say something soon, before Mama starts asking questions in front of him."

"What about Cass's family, Em? How do they feel about this?"

Emmie gave her sister a blank stare.

"What? They don't know?"

She didn't answer.

"They do know and they're all okay with it?"

"I…I don't really know. I don't know much about them," she admitted. "Cass grew up in Abilene."

"How'd she end up out here?"

"Her mom, I guess. Her mother's family is all Lute's from Merkel and Trent. Her grandmother still lives there."

Cora sat back in the booth and slouched a little. "The long-horn farm?"

"Yeah, what's left of it, anyway…the stock I mean. They've still got all the land," she said, as she thought about the potential of a wind farm being there, "but they've sold most of their livestock."

"So, it's Cass and her grandmother? I'm confused."

"No, no. Cass manages that for her grandmother, but she has her own little place now…just bought it."

"She said Jimmie is her nephew, at the game."

"He's her sister Pam's son. She's in Abilene. That's all I really know. She's only ever talked about her grandmother, her sister and the kids. I don't know where her mother is now or if she ever sees her. I got the impression that was a sore subject, so I didn't pry. I don't know anything about her father or any other siblings. I assume there are none since there's no one else to help with the ranch."

Cora eyed her sister but said nothing.

Emmie looked at her and then looked away. "You think I'm moving too fast, don't you?"

"No…yes," Cora began. "It's not for me to decide. It's just… you barely know her. I mean, how many times have you been out with her…sat and talked, even?"

Emmie blushed.

"Em!"

"It's…it's different with her, okay. I just know. When we're together…in the same room even…"

"Pardon me for being blunt, but are you sure it's not just lust?"

Her head shot up. "It's not!" She blew out a breath. *I really need to talk to Cass.*

CHAPTER 15

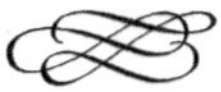

Thursday Evening, November 10th

"I'm glad you could come over for a little while," Cass said. She pulled Emmie into her arms, dipped her head and touched her lips to the shorter woman's.

Emmie started to return the kiss, but then groaned and pulled back.

Cass gave her an odd look. "Something wrong?"

"I…we…I can't stay tonight."

"I didn't expect you to. I didn't expect you to come over at all, on a school night," she teased. When Emmie didn't react, she released her hold on her and took a step back. "What else is going through that head of yours?"

"I…can we talk?"

"Oh…"

Emmie waved a hand. "It's not bad…it's just there are things we should talk about, is all."

"Okay." Cass took Emmie's hand and led her to the sofa. She

waited while she sat and then took a chair adjacent to her. "It still sounds pretty serious. Are you having second thoughts, maybe?"

"Cass…no. I told you it's not that bad. I'm just trying to deal with my family…my mom, especially. She thinks this is all an experiment." Emmie said, as she made air quotes.

Cass winced. "I'm sorry to hear that."

"What about your family? You never talk about them. How are they going to take this? I mean, have you even told anyone?"

"I've uh…I've actually talked to my sister about you moving in here. She's fine with it all, but then, she's always known about me. And Jimmy? As long as we keep him fed, he won't care one way or another."

That made Emmie smile, but she was still worried. "What about your parents? Any other brothers and sisters? You've only talked about your grandmother."

"It's just me and Pam. Mom's in Abilene. She, let's say, struggles with reality. She's been in and out of rehab centers for the past ten years, since my dad left."

"Drugs?"

Cass nodded. "Alcohol, pain killers. You name it."

"So, you don't see your father much?"

She shook her head. "Hardly ever saw him when he was with mom. He's a long-haul trucker; oil tankers. He pulls from the refineries and drives loads east, into Ohio and Pennsylvania. He's got a tiny apartment in Abilene that he's in maybe one day, a day and a half a week."

"So, there were no male heirs to the Lute family farms?"

"No, not hardly. Gram and Gramps had three girls. Two married and moved away. One of them is gone now and my mom may as well be."

"That's pretty harsh."

"It's reality. She helped a little before my father left but, even then, not much. He used to drive shorter hauls, be home every couple or three days, overnight. She was all wrapped up in being the happy homemaker and making him happy when he was there. He couldn't have cared less."

"Do you ever talk to him at all?"

"Sometimes, not much," Cass admitted. "He was very hands off, as far back as I can remember, even when he was home for a long weekend or a holiday. The money he made paid for my high school sports and put me through college but, he really had very little to do with me or Pam growing up. He didn't even walk Pam down the aisle at her wedding. He sure hasn't offered any sort of support since her divorce. He never sees his grandkids."

It was Emmie's turn to feel the need to offer comfort. She pulled Cass into an embrace and they held each other for several long seconds.

Cass pulled back. "As for my grandmother, I've actually suggested she leave her own place and come and live with me."

"Really? Sell the family ranch?"

"No, no. Nothing that drastic. Our places are so close together, it would be easy for me and Jimmy to continue to manage both. Quite frankly, that boy is going to have to man up some day and pull more weight."

Emmie stayed quiet. She thought Jimmy was coming along just fine, but Cass knew him better.

"Gran is resisting leaving her own home, even though she's struggling with her health. Her hip seems fine, but her blood pressure is up a lot and so is her sugar." She trailed off and stared at the wall over Emmie's shoulder, lost in thought.

"Penny for them."

The rancher shook her head to clear it. "It's nothing. Just worried about her is all."

Emmie wasn't convinced. She tilted her head and looked into her lover's eyes. "What aren't you telling me?" she whispered.

Cass sighed. "There's no putting one over on you, is there? I have a gut feeling her blood pressure issues are stress related."

"Over me, right?"

Cass looked away. "Us. Look, Em, she's known that I'm gay for years. I just…I never flaunted it; never brought anyone home. Never had anyone that I wanted to bring home, you know?" She leaned across the open space between them and picked up Emmie's hand. "Now that it's happening, that you're moving in, I'm just worried she's stressing over it. That she's not quite as open minded as I thought."

"Maybe we should rethink this whole thing…"

Cass stood and pulled Emmie up with her then put her hands-on Emmie's shoulders and pulled her close. "No. I'm worried about her, but that doesn't change how I feel about you. I want you here, Em. I need you here."

CHAPTER 16

Thursday, November 24th
Thanksgiving
The Oakes Family Ranch

Emmie looked up and down the long table. Her father sat at the head, as usual. And, also as usual, her mother's seat to his immediate left was vacant. She was off in the kitchen fetching more of this and that. It was quiet. Too quiet. She glanced at the other table, set up to the left, and watched as Tyler ruffled Seth's hair, drawing his attention to him, while their 13-year-old cousin Kenny Jr. Stole a big forkful of her son's mashed potatoes. *At least the kids are having a good time.*

Seth Jr. Caught the movement out of the corner of his eye. He spun around and called to her, "Mom! Ty and Kenny are messing with me! Why can't they sit at the big table with you guys?"

Dusty shook a finger at his older grandchildren and admonished them to leave the little ones alone. He looked down the table at his adult children and their spouses. "Cat got everyone's tongues? There's a big playoff game tomorrow night, isn't that right Fred?" He tipped his head toward the other table. "Tyler? I know you all have been watching film all week. What do we know about this Glen Rose team?"

Emmie relaxed a little as the males around both tables started talking football, but she didn't let her guard all the way down. Eventually, her mind wandered to Cass. She'd tried to invite her, but Cass thought it was better that they wait to do family holidays together, as a couple until they were living together as a couple.

She stifled a shudder. She couldn't see Christmas, right around the corner, being much better than the, up until that moment, sullen affair she'd been enduring. Her mother hadn't hesitated to tell her brothers and their wives of her plans. None had said anything negative, but they hadn't shown any support for her either. *What did I expect?*

WHEN HER SISTER'S-IN-LAW were out of earshot, Emmie leaned toward Cora who stood at the sink performing the annual after Thanksgiving dinner, pot scrubbing ritual. "I wasn't going to move out until the Christmas break at both schools, but if it's going to be like this for the next month..."

Cora looked over her shoulder and then back at her sister. "You're going to move now?"

"May as well. It can't get any worse around here."

"It might if you leave now, Em." She glanced over her shoulder again and then whispered, "What about Seth?"

"He's staying here for now, like I promised. I won't move him in over there until after Christmas."

Cora shook her head.

* * *

Friday, November 25th
Graham, Texas

EMMIE STARED at Cass's back, a few rows below them. Cass had sketched a wave in her direction when she and the woman and the young girl with her took their seats. Emmie assumed the other two were her sister and niece, but she didn't dare go down and open that can of worms in front of most of her family, arrayed around her in stands.

Everyone was pretty wound up about the game. She was trying to be positive, but it had been a long day. She'd called Cass and told her what she was planning and, after hearing words of encouragement from her, she took the plunge and told her parents and her son before they'd left on the drive to Graham.

Having Seth there had softened the confrontation a little. She knew that wouldn't last. She figured her mother was biting her tongue, biding her time, in deference to the boy.

Seth had been full of questions. He remembered Cass and said he really liked her. Em had smiled at that. He barely knew her but, he'd seen her in action and, in his young mind, he knew all he needed to know.

She was patient and tried to answer everything Seth asked. Her dad had given her a little space to talk to the boy, but her mother had stubbornly hovered nearby as they talked. She guffawed loudly when he said he was curious to see the ranch Cass owned and to meet Jimmy. He wasn't concerned for a minute about her not moving him with her after the holidays, but he was blunt in his six-year-old assessment of what starting at a new school the following year would entail.

"What about my friends?" he'd asked.

Trudy had shot her a look then; an I told you so look.

"Since we live way out here right now, you have mostly school friends. You'll make new friends pretty fast over at the Merkle elementary school."

He tipped his head and gave that a second's worth of thought and then nodded, everything settled in his young mind.

A cheer went up in the stands as everyone jumped to their feet. She got up a little slower and tried to focus on the team entering the stadium.

CHAPTER 17

Tuesday Evening, December 6th

Emmie smiled as Jimmy cleaned his plate and jumped up to serve himself seconds from the baking dish she'd left cooling on top of the stove.

"Slow down boy," Cass bellowed at him. "Leave some for our lunches tomorrow. You'd think no one ever fed you."

Emmie told Jimmy, "Take all you want. There's a second pan for lunches."

Cass shot her a look.

"What? I was planning ahead."

"You're spoiling him is what you're doing, making him soft. They're still in the playoffs, you know?"

"He's gotta keep his strength up then, Cass." She gave Jimmy a conspiratorial look as he sat back down with another heaping plateful of her Aztec chicken casserole.

"I like nights when the two of you don't have class."

"Because she cooks?" Cass asked. "I cook."

Emmie coughed a little and cleared her throat.

Cass shot her another look. "I do."

"Sandwiches ain't cooking," Jimmy said.

"Aren't," Emmie supplied. If the teenager caught the correction, he didn't respond.

"Jimmy has really taken to you," Cass said as they were cleaning up.

Emmie had three containers lined up on the island top. She carefully spooned the chicken dish into each one.

Cass quirked an eyebrow. "Only three?"

"Seth won't eat it. He says it's too spicy. I'll make him a sandwich." She thought for a second and then asked, "There's still quite a bit. Do you think your grandmother would like some?"

"Probably not. She's never been much of a chicken fan. If you want to send extra along with me though, you can." Cass said, her tone hopeful. "You okay?" she asked, when the other woman didn't respond.

Emmie gave her a small smile. "Yeah. I just miss Seth. I mean, I see him at school, but it's weird not having homework time with him and story time..." Her voice trailed away, and she stared off, her eyes distant.

Cass moved behind her, wrapped her arms around her waist and put her chin on Emmie's shoulder. "You're not regretting moving in, are you?"

Emmie shook herself and turned to face Cass. "No...no. I love it here. I love what we have together...how we're learning about each other. I'd just like Seth to be here now too. I didn't think that through. I should have stood my ground."

Cass bit her tongue. She had her own struggles with her grandmother. She was worried about her, but Rosa Lute had a mind of her own and she wasn't taking advice or criticism from anyone that she didn't ask for. Instead she asked, "Will he be able to come over and spend the weekend?"

"Seth? I should hope so. My mother doesn't need to be dreaming up any more stuff to keep him there, instead of letting him come here. I should have put my foot down on that; don't you think?"

Cass figured she was the last person who should be giving that sort of advice. She gave Emmie a little nod and pulled her to her for a kiss.

Emmie's cell phone buzzed where it lay on the counter.

"Leave it," Cass whispered.

Emmie half turned out of the embrace and glanced at the screen. "It's my mom. It may be about Seth."

Cass dropped her arms and went back to the dishes in the sink while Emmie answered.

"Hello mama. Is everything okay?"

"No. Everything is not okay." Trudy's tone was haughty.

Emmie drew in a long breath. "Let me rephrase that; is Seth okay?"

"He's fine. Missing his mother."

"Let me talk to him."

"He's down at the barn with your father. That's not why I called."

Of course not.

"I want to talk to you about Christmas."

"We've already discussed that. As much as it pains me to be separated from him, and believe me, it does, I promised Seth could stay there until just after Christmas, remember?"

Cass put the baking dish she'd finished cleaning into the rack to dry, then signaled Emmie that she'd take over the lunch making duties. It sounded to her like their conversation was going to get heated. When she heard Trudy's voice come back over Emmie's phone she knew she was right. She waved Emmie out of the room, so she could have it out with her mother privately.

"I know that," Trudy was saying, "and I hope you'll keep your word."

"Of course." Emmie waited a beat. She knew there was more to it than that.

"I'm just concerned, is all."

"About?"

"About what you are and aren't going to do for the holidays, and beyond. I realize you plan on moving Seth right after Christmas, whether he likes it or not."

Emmie covered the receiver and sighed.

Trudy Oakes railed on. "But what about the traditional family Christmas Eve and Christmas Day gatherings? Where are you going to be? Are you really going to buck all of our traditions? I mean, poor Seth. He's innocent in all of this."

"Mother, I fully intend to be there for Christmas Eve. That's were Seth will be. I'm not going to not be with him."

"And Christmas morning?"

She hadn't thought that out. "I'll work that out. You'll have a house full. I may leave late, come back here and just come over early enough for the big hullabaloo in the morning."

"Emmie Lou, you watch your mouth! Don't call it that."

"Sorry Mama…"

* * *

CASS WALKED up behind Emmie where she sat at the desk they'd set up for her in the living room. "What are you up too?"

Emmie rubbed at her temples. "I'm trying to grade spelling homework."

"Not going so well?"

She shook her head.

"Your mom?"

"Yes."

"Do you want to talk about it?" Cass started to rub her shoulders. "You're so tense."

"There's not much to say. She called here to poke, prod and guilt me into spending the whole holiday over there. She says, 'it's tradition'."

"You can, you know. I don't want to interfere with the holidays this year. Next year…that's different. We'll have a whole year to figure it out and come up with a plan that considers everyone."

Emmie rolled her shoulders. "This should be the other way around. I should be giving you a massage rub after the day you've put in."

Cass smiled but didn't stop. She pressed her thumbs into the knot at the base of Emmie's neck and worked at the knot there.

Emmie moaned. "Wow…or you could just keep doing that."

Slowly, the knot started to dissipate. Cass rubbed her a little bit more and then bent down and kissed her neck in the spot she'd been tending to before moving around to the curve of Em's neck and shoulder and feathering kisses along it as she inched her blouse away."

Emmie drew in a deep breath.

Emboldened, Cass straightened up and ran the hand now around her lover's upper arm, down to cup a breast. She rubbed her thumb lightly over the areola.

Emmie moaned, all thoughts of the work still to be done, gone.

Cass pulled her up out of her chair and turned her. She dipped her head and was about to kiss her when a heavy footfall clattered across the front porch toward the door. They stepped apart just as the door opened and Jimmy entered.

. . .

In the bedroom, an hour later, Cass pulled Emmie into a deep kiss, picking up where she left off. When she managed to drag her lips away, she worked the buttons on Em's blouse. "I can't believe you stayed in your school clothes. Let's get you into something a little more comfortable."

Emmie gave her a sidelong look. "Bed?"

"Exactly."

Em couldn't help but laugh. She stood waiting while Cass took off everything but her panties and then she returned the favor, but completely undressed the other woman.

Cass gave Em a longing look then gathered her in close and walked her backward toward the bed.

The heat of the taller woman's body made Emmie groan. As Cass followed her down and covered her body with her own, she lost herself in what she was feeling.

CHAPTER 18

Wednesday, December 7th

Emmie gave herself the once over in the mirror. She blew out a breath and contemplated the image she saw. She could see dark circles under her eyes. *All the sleep in the world won't relieve this stress.*

She sighed, turned and stepped into her shoes, always the last thing she put on before facing a day on her feet, corralling young children and trying to teach them everything they needed to know to pass on to the next grade.

Cass called out from the kitchen, "I'm out the door, Em. You better shake a leg too, if you don't want to be late."

She stepped around the corner in time for the last couple of words and smiled at Cass as she stepped into her boots. "I love you."

Cass grinned at her and said, "I love you too. Now, since you're done fussing and primping for those pre-teen students of yours, how about a kiss goodbye for me?"

"Of course." Emmie moved over to the taller woman and grinned as she knocked her Stetson back with a couple of fingers then leaned toward her with fish lips for a kiss.

Emmie made a face. "How about a proper kiss to start the day?" She took hold of the sides of the Carhartt jacket Cass wore and pulled her toward her.

Cass dipped her head and touched her lips to Emmie's

Emmie wished they could stay this way for hours, but all too soon, it was over. They both had work to do.

Moments later, she was settled into her car to make the drive to Sweetwater. She tried to count in her head, how many more times she would drive West for work instead of East, to Abilene. She'd given notice to the administration at the school. She wondered how long it would be before word of her departure circulated. That got her thinking about her move. She hadn't informed the administration that she'd moved out of Sweetwater and given them her new address.

Just wait till word gets out where I'm living and who I'm living with. That could get ugly. She shook her head. *Think positive! Don't worry about what those people think. Worry about yourself, Cass and getting settled in. Worry about Seth...not about them. Nothing I say or do is going to change their minds about anything anyway.*

* * *

CASS SLAMMED the post hole diggers into the ground one more time. Her lips set in a grim line, she glanced down the length of the fence. It was the third time this week a bull had tried to knock through to get to the cows and had a post loose. She was tired of fixing fence.

She let her mind wander to other things. The term was almost over at school. Soon, Emmie wouldn't be in class anymore. She'd have the data she needed to support the defense of her master's Thesis and she'd be preparing even harder for that.

Other things were moving faster than she expected too. *I like having her around, and I'm sure it will be better for her once Seth is here full time too. I just wonder how Seth is going to handle it all.*

Though she didn't dare say it out loud, or even think it around Emmie, Cass wondered if Trudy Oakes was poisoning the pot, filling Seth's head full of nonsense about moving and losing all of his friends.

She sighed as her mind continued to wander, alighting on her grandmother, as it often did. Her mobility issues were becoming a bigger concern. She decided she'd try and talk with her about it at lunch and this time she wasn't going to let the stubborn old woman give her the brush off.

"It's good chili, Gran."

"Not too spicy? You know I just don't taste it right these days."

Cass shook her head. "It's just right." When Rosa Lute turned to tend to the pot on the stove, Cass took a big bite of cornbread to try and cool the heat of the chili peppers.

"It's cool out there today," her grandmother was saying. "Wanted to make something to warm you up."

"You don't have to make me lunch. I usually pack something along with me, you know?"

The old woman flipped a hand at her dismissively. "Leftovers or a sandwich. Nothing fresh made, from scratch."

Cass started to tell her that about the amazing chicken casserole Emmie had concocted the previous night, but she thought better of it. That was a battle for another day. Instead she asked, "Are you going to eat?"

Rosa hobbled about, using the counter tops for support, not answering.

"Gran, sit and eat with me. Take a load off and let's talk."

The older woman stopped midway between the stove and the refrigerator and gave Cass a look as she braced her hands on the back of a chair. "About what?" Her look and tone were suspicious.

Cass realized she hadn't thought a good approach all the way through. The old woman was sharp. She'd see right through any attempt to soften things or hide what she was really thinking. She plunged ahead. "About the ranch, Gran. What we're doing. What we've been doing."

Rosa sat. "What's wrong now?"

"Nothing's wrong. Everything is going pretty well." *Other than a couple of horny bulls…* "It's just, I'm concerned about your health and how much you can really do. You're barely getting around."

Rosa started to rise.

"Don't get up. I know what you're doing. You're going to say that everything is fine, it's just the chill in the air. It's not though, is it?"

The older woman looked away but then turned back and leaned across the table toward her granddaughter. "I'm not getting any younger, you know? It's been a hard life, working this spread, all these years. I admit, I've lost a step or two, but I'm not ready to be put out to pasture yet."

Cass groaned inwardly. "That's not what I'm saying. What I'm getting at is, Jimmy's got half a year of school left. In all honesty, he's not ready to take over the day to day stuff that I do now, when he does finish and, admit this, you can't help. We can't afford to hire any hands other than maybe someone to come in during baling season. We've got this big plan to bring a wind energy program here and have me run that but then what? Who runs what's left of your ranch and mine while he's still mired in his learning curve and his attitude?"

"You don't want the windmills, now?"

"I didn't say that." Cass rubbed the stress knot at the back of her neck, her lunch getting cold in front of her, forgotten. "What I'm saying is, between the two ranches, as they are right now, with me and Jimmy doing all the work, we'll eat and make enough to pay the bills. Being in the wind energy program would be a nice income for the family, but at the cost of keeping Jimmy on track and of almost all of your tillable, grazable land. Is that what you really want?"

Rosa put her hands flat against the table and looked Cass in the eye as she spoke. "It's hard for me, with my health, yes. That's why I want to do this. I've thought long and hard about it. I want to make sure to have the money to not be a burden as my health declines even more."

Cass felt horrible. She reached out for her grandmother's hand. "You're not a burden to anyone, and you never will be."

"That thought aside, there's also the fact that I want something to leave to you kids. You, your sister, your sister's kids and any kids you may…maybe someday, have." The old woman raised a hand to stop Cass from speaking. "I know what you're going to say but hear me out. You love that woman, I get that. She has a child. The two of you may want more. Lord knows, there's dozens of ways to come about putting a family together these days that don't involve men. I don't pretend to understand it, but it is what it is."

Cass was shocked, but she recovered quickly. "I was about to say that it isn't necessary to leave me anything. I have what I need, and Emmie and her son will be well taken care of."

The old woman shook her head. "You don't understand child. It's what your grandfather wanted; his dying wish. He wanted to see the family provided for. Ranching isn't going to get us very far now-a-days; not without him. Wind will."

CHAPTER 19

Thursday, December 8th

As the last of her students filed into the lunchroom, Emmie turned on her heels and made a beeline for the teacher's lounge. She'd missed breakfast in the mad scramble to find her keys. Her stomach rumbled the whole time she'd tried to teach her young charges long division in the last period.

She could hear the hum of conversation as she approached the lounge. She walked in smiling and looked around at all the faces. The room grew quiet. Everyone looked her way and then away.

Emmie felt the heat rise up her neck and across her cheeks. Knowing they'd been talking about her, she spun toward the refrigerator and tried to hide her embarrassed blush.

She heard a couple of the others get up and leave, their breaks over. She grabbed the bag with her sandwich in it and turned to face the remaining members of the group.

As she contemplated whether to take a seat at the table or in one of the easy chairs on the opposite wall, her friend and fellow fourth grade teacher, Patrice entered the room.

"Hey," Patrice addressed her first, "just getting in here too?" She rambled on before Emmie could say anything. "I swear, I'm going to put out collection jars at the stores for lunch money donations. If one more kid forgets…"

Emmie shook her head no, but she smiled. "I don't think they're the forgetful ones."

Patrice headed toward the easy chairs and Emmie followed.

While Emmie unwrapped her turkey on wheat, Patrice opened the little cooler bag she kept in her desk drawer and started to remove her own food, but her eyes were on her coworker. "So, tell me; is the rumor true?"

EYEBROWS RAISED, Emmie felt the blush creeping back. She didn't dare look at the teachers still sitting around the table, listening to every word. "I…I…what rumor is that?"

"You know; the one where you're leaving us at the end of this school year." Patrice asked.

"Oh. You heard."

"Um hmm. So, where are you headed? Please don't tell me you're leaving teaching. You're too good at it."

"I'm not. I'll uh, be finished with my master's by the break, other than my thesis. Then I'll be teaching college level math at the little branch campus Texas Tech has in Abilene for pre-med students."

"College? Wow! There's a switch."

The mummers among the others in the room picked back up then. Emmie knew that her leaving or where she was going hadn't been the original topic of conversation. Now they just had more fuel for the speculative fire.

Patrice gave her a look.

Emmie looked away, but she caught Patrice's whispered, "There's more to it, isn't there?" loud and clear.

She whispered back, "Later."

PATRICE DUCKED INTO THE RESTROOM, leaving Emmie to walk back to the fourth-grade hallway alone. "Em, wait up," Barbara Shone, called out. She touched Emmie's shoulder as she came alongside and leaned in.

"I know why you're really leaving."

Emmie gave her a look but didn't respond.

"You're with a…a woman now, right? I mean, it's not my business and it's not anybody else's business either, but word's floating around, you know?"

"You're right. My personal life isn't anyone's business."

Barbara dropped her hand. "Hey, I'm on your side here, okay?" She smiled and gave Emmie a little nod.

Emmie let out a heavy breath then whispered back, "That's not why I'm leaving, Barb. I've always wanted to teach college."

The other woman leaned closer again. "Here's the thing; I don't know what the Principal knows or doesn't know, but… watch your back, you know? He's not going to be on your side."

"What's the worst he can do? I've already resigned. I'm done at the end of the school year."

"That's just it. Remember that morals clause you signed when you started with the district?" She didn't wait for an answer. "You wouldn't be the first teacher they drummed over the head and out with it."

* * *

"YOU JUST PASSED ME DEAR. I was coming out of the salon."

"In the middle of the day, Mama?"

"Ronald Brownman's calling hours are this evening. Did you forget?"

Of course. Any public appearance meant Trudy had to look just so. "Oh. No, no. I'll be there to pay my respects."

"I figured you'd just stay in town, maybe come out to spend some time with Seth, before the viewing."

"I'm not taking Seth to the viewing, Mama. It would traumatize him and, besides, he barely knew the man."

"That's not what I meant."

I know what you meant.

"I thought we could talk a little more about Christmas too. Make some plans."

"We've talked about that."

"Well, things have changed since then. We've got a couple of more people coming to spend Christmas Eve now. Your aunt and uncle will be in from Arizona. They'll want to spend time with you."

"They haven't wanted to in years. They've never even met Seth Junior."

Her mother blew out a heavy breath. "Why do you have to be so difficult?"

CHAPTER 20

Cass eyed Emmie all through dinner, knowing something was bothering her, but she didn't dare ask until Jimmy was done and out of earshot.

"You put on a brave face, all through dinner, but you seem awfully low. What's up?" Cass asked her when the teenager had rinsed his plate and gone on his way.

Emmie shrugged. "It's nothing…nothing you or I can do anything about, anyway."

"Your mom, again?"

She tipped her head and gave Cass a sidelong look. "Her too, now that you mention it, but her guilt trips are nothing compared to everything else."

"Em, tell me."

Emmie told Cass about what happened at school. "And then, to make matters worse, like you figured, I had another go around with Mama about Christmas over the phone, on my way home. She's upset, railing on about how the big family Christmas Eve bash is going by the wayside because of me leaving and me taking Seth away and over Cora being so upset with her over her inability to accept what's happened. She just goes on and on. I'm supposed to go to calling hours for an old family friend tonight. Even under the best of circumstances, I don't want to, but to make it worse..."

"She'll be there?" Cass asked.

"Yes. Holding court and saying heaven knows what to whom."

"I don't know what to say about that. I'd certainly go with you, if you want, but I don't think my being there would help."

Emmie sighed. "Thanks. I appreciate that, but you're probably right."

"I hate to say this, but we tend to have our family gathering on Christmas Eve now too. It isn't as elaborate as what your folks do these days, by the sounds of it. There's church and then usually... in years past, we all gathered at Gran's; me, her, my sister, the kids and usually any hands we still had and their families, if they wanted to come. This year, it will probably be just the family."

"That sounds nice actually, but it does sort of prove my mother's point. Going forward, I'm going to want to spend holidays with you. I don't know what I'll do. I suppose I'll ride it out this year and see what develops next year. We have a few other family holidays to get through between now and then."

Cass nodded her agreement, but she stared off at a wall, seeming far away.

"What are you thinking about?" Emmie asked, gently.

She shuddered slightly as she answered, "Paps. Things were a lot different when he was with us, especially at Christmas. We used to have these parties...always the Saturday before Christmas Eve. Everybody came. Aunts and uncles, cousins, all the hands and their families, neighbors from off down the road...everybody.

"Even your mom?"

"Usually, yeah...depending on her condition and where she was at the time. When she was in rehab..." She trailed off.

Emmie changed the subject. "Why'd you quit having those?"

"We had one the year after he died, and everyone still came but then, after that...I don't know. I don't know if Gran's heart just wasn't in it or if everyone just drifted away. For the last couple of years, we've just done Christmas Eve." She got that far away look in her eyes again.

Em let her be and got up to clear the table. As she scrubbed the pots, her own thoughts turned to Christmas's past, even before Seth Jr. came along. What Cass had described was like her own experience. There had always been big parties at the ranch when they were kids, just before the holiday. They'd stopped when her brothers had families of their own, in-laws and other obligations. Now, Christmas Eve was all that was left.

She whirled around and, leaning back against the sink, she said, "I was just thinking about traditions we've let go out at our ranch too. We used to have a big Christmas bash too, but it's been seven or eight years ago since the last one."

"They get too expensive?"

"No...at least, I don't think so." She told Cass about her brothers and their families. "That's why they said we weren't doing them anymore."

"So, traditions do change on the Oakes spread?"

"That, they do," Emmie said. "Maybe it's time to start a new one that includes everybody."

Cass gave her a puzzled look.

"What if we had a party somewhere neutral...or not...it's short notice...I'm just throwing ideas out there, and we invited everybody? My family, your family, their families, in-laws, friends, neighbors, classmates...everybody?"

"For Christmas Eve?"

Em wrinkled her nose and thought. "Maybe not Christmas Eve. More like how both of our families used to do it, just prior."

"I don't know. Maybe. It would be short notice for a lot of people."

"For this year yes, but what do you say we do it anyway and get something started?"

Cass twisted in her chair and looked at the calendar hanging on the wall behind her. "You do realize, today is already the 8th," she said, looking back over her shoulder. "When did you have in mind?"

"How about Saturday, the 17th?"

Cass chuckled and shook her head. "A week or so away? And I'm still in class to boot? There's no way, unless you put it together all yourself, Em."

"The 23rd then? It's not a Saturday…that's Christmas Eve, but it's a Friday and most people will be off for the holidays by then, able to travel around a little and still get back in time to their own family plans. That gives us a good two weeks to put it together and get the word out for anyone that wants to come."

"And can," Cass put in. "We probably won't get a big crowd but that could work. Do you really think we have the room to do a big bash here, though?"

Emmie looked around with a critical eye and shrugged. "Not seated for a dinner, but if we clear some furniture and make it like an open house? People coming and going? They're probably going to have more than one place to visit that night, being so close to Christmas Eve and all."

"Maybe so," Cass said, nodding. She put a hand to her chin and leaned into the table, thinking. Out of the blue, she said, "While you're at calling hours, I'll go see Gran. Her place is bigger, and this might be just the thing she needs. She's a heck of a planner, that's for sure."

"Hmm, okay. Do you really think she'll want to do this…especially with us?"

"Let me ask you, do you really think your family will come?"

Emmie gave that some thought. "I can't honestly say whether my mom will. Probably. Her curiosity might get the best of her. Cora will be here with her crew."

"If they don't have plans," Cass put in.

"No. I know my sister. She'll be here."

"And your brothers and their families?"

"Maybe...probably. There'll be food, so there's a good chance."

Jimmy wandered into the kitchen then. "Talking about a party? If there's food, I'm there. That always wins me over."

CHAPTER 21

Thursday, December 15th

So close to Christmas, the hallways were always bedlam. Teachers tried to control peaceful movements from their classrooms to the art room, the music room and the gym, but there was only so much you could do with boisterous five to eight-year old children, focused this year a scant ten days ahead to the looming holiday.

As she tried to herd her own group of twenty-five to the den of the art teacher, Mrs. McMorris, she maneuvered past one of the second-grade teachers she had mentored and coached just a few years before. She smiled at Michael Hull and dipped her head in an acknowledging nod. He looked away from her and then spun halfway around to face the line of his students going the opposite way down the hall, back toward their classroom.

"Don't dawdle," he called out to a couple of stragglers. "There's spelling to do!"

Emmie knew he'd intentionally avoided her. He hadn't been

stopping into her room in the afternoons on his way out to say hello and talk about this and that as he often did.

The word was getting out and it wasn't pretty. No one save Patrice and maybe Barbara Shone seemed to be on her side. She wasn't too sure about Barbara.

Emmie wondered how long it would be before parents started finding out. She thought about the playoff game the next night. She figured she'd get a few looks from parents there. It seemed like everyone was talking about heading to Arlington for the game now that the administration was closing school early to allow for people who wanted to go to have enough time to travel to the stadium more than three hours away. She figured many classrooms would be half empty on Friday anyway.

SHE MADE sure all her students got on their buses and then spent a couple of minutes with Seth before her dad picked him up on his way through town.

"You're coming home with me this weekend."

"But I want to go to Tyler's game tomorrow. That's all Ritchie's been talking about all day, Mom. He keeps telling me how *his* brother is going to whoop on some West Orange butts."

"Seth! That's not very polite."

"Well it's true, isn't it? The Mustangs are going to win, aren't they?"

Against the reigning state champs? "There are no guarantees buddy, but I sure hope they do. I'm sure they'll play their hardest."

The boy nodded, satisfied with that answer until he remembered his original statement. "What about the game? I really want to go."

"Since when are you so interested in football?"

Seth gave her a look askance. "Everybody in Texas likes football, Mom."

Somebody has been feeding him the age-old line...my dad, my broth-

ers, his friends...could be anybody. She let him off the hook. "We're going, so you can let up, okay? Grandma will bring you to school in the morning and Grandpa will pick us both up from here. We'll go to the game and then ride back with Cass from Arlington."

"She's not staying there like Grandma and Grandpa?"

"No sweetie. There are animals to take care of and other things that need to be done in the morning. We have to get back to the ranch."

Before he could ask another question, Dusty Oakes pulled up in his pickup and gave them a wave. She waved back, gave Seth a quick hug and then headed back to her classroom once he was on his way.

SHE WAS GRADING math homework assignments from the night before when the speaker over the door buzzed and the Principals secretary called out to her.

"Yes?"

"Dr. Deaton would like to see you in his office, before you go...before you leave."

This can't be good. She took a deep breath. "Okay. Please tell him I'll be down there in a few minutes."

"Very well." The speaker popped as the PA system cut back out.

Emmie scratched a check minus on the top of the incomplete paper in front of her then gathered all the work up into her math folder and stowed it away in a drawer. Unnerved, she didn't have the focus to finish them. She stood, smoothed her dress, gathered her things then drew in a deep breath before marching off down the hall to Kenneth Deaton's office to face whatever fire he was going to bring to bear.

Beatrice Stowe, a fixture at secretary since Emmie herself had attended grade school in the building, was on her feet, gathering her own things when she walked into the administrative offices. The gray-haired woman glanced at her, shook her head then looked away as she slipped on her coat.

Once upon a time, Emmie had liked the woman, thinking her kindly. Now, as she approached seventy and continued to work, she'd become a cross and crotchety sort of person. Rumor had it, the school board was going to force her into retirement at the end of the school year. "Should I just go on in?" Emmie asked her.

Beatrice waved an arm toward Deaton's office and marched out the door, brushing past her.

Emmie steeled herself, stepped up to the door marked Kenneth Deaton, Ph. D. - Principal and knocked softly. She didn't wait for a response before entering. *Let's just get this over with, already!*

Deaton, a heavyset man with a penchant for three-piece suits, didn't waste any time. She wasn't even in the chair he'd indicated she should take when he said, "I've heard a rumor and I want to know if it's true." He pulled a handkerchief out of his breast pocket and mopped at his brow.

"I've given you my resignation and plenty of notice, Dr. Deaton. What else do you need?"

He shook a finger at her. "Don't play dumb with me. We both know that's not what this is about." He crumpled the kerchief and jammed it into his suit coat pocket.

She waited, silent. *I'm not volunteering anything.*

He stared across his desk at her and then gave in. "Am I to understand that you're living with a woman as...as..." He trailed off, unsure how to phrase the rest of his question.

She quirked an eyebrow at him. "As what?"

"Are you, or are you not living in sin with another woman?"

She boiled at his tone and his obvious distaste. *This can't be headed anywhere good, no matter what I say.* She thought about getting up and marching out and never looking back. Choosing a different tack, she asked instead, "Is there a reason you assume I'm living with a woman, 'in sin'?"

He leaned over his desk and steepled his hands. "I see what you're doing. Stop turning this in circles. Is she your mother? Your sister? No. She's not. There's no logical...no acceptable reason for you to be...to be living with this woman."

"Let me put this another way then, Dr. Deaton; who I live with is none of your business."

"Whom."

That's what he zeros in on? She rose. "Who, whom...how about, as my students say, whatever." Where I live, as long as it's in a county contiguous with the school district, is my choice. Good day." She turned to exit.

"Wait," he said, holding up a hand. "We're not finished here."

Oh, I think we are! She stopped and turned back toward him, but she didn't resume her seat.

He rose also. "I can't have belligerence from my staff and immoral behavior modeled for the students. I'll speak with the board. I'll be recommending you be dismissed and replaced."

Emmie's spirits deflated. "There's...there's no reason for that. I've done nothing to give any student...any parent pause. Nothing at all."

"You're living with another woman in a...in a...a clandestine, sordid relationship. The damage has already been done whether you admit to it or not." The finger shook at her again. "Do I need to remind you, we have a code of conduct here, which you signed?"

"I'll be gone at the end of the school year. You can replace me then with anyone you want to."

"That's not good enough. I have students to consider and their irate parents!"

"How long do I have?" Emmie asked. Her voice sounded hollow, even to her.

"There isn't a board meeting scheduled until after the break. If

I had my way about it, you'd be on administrative leave effective immediately, but appropriate subs are in short supply right now." He rounded his desk and moved toward her as he said, "You'll work out the semester and keep your private life to yourself. You're not to come onto school property with that woman or attend school related functions elsewhere with her. Do I make myself clear?"

"Oh, crystal," Emmie shot back.

"You'll want to be at the next board meeting. You have a right to be heard."

Funny you should mention it since your mind is already made up... Emmie turned on her heel and left.

Patrice caught up with her halfway to her car. "What's got you moving like a ball of fire?"

Emmie shook her head at her friend and kept moving.

"Em? You can tell me anything. You know that, right?"

She sighed as she slowed her step. She wanted to run right to Cass, but she thought, *she'll be working, and this is my battle.*

Patrice was still talking. "Em? Whatever it is, you can unload it on me. I'm here to listen."

"There isn't anything you can do to help me."

"Maybe, maybe not. I can be your sounding board though... unless there's someone else for that?"

Emmie knew she was blushing, but she didn't say anything.

"You said we'd talk later, Em. It's later."

She glanced at her friend. "Okay. But not here."

"I LIVE WITH CASS...CASSANDRA, but she prefers Cass. I met her at the college during my TA assignment for my master's thesis," Emmie half whispered.

Patrice sat on the other side of the booth with both hands wrapped around her coffee cup, nodding along to Emmie's words.

"You're acting like you knew," Emmie accused.

"I knew you were with a woman," Patrice whispered back. "I just didn't have the particulars. The rumor mill hadn't gotten quite that far."

"Shockingly. They've been talking about me for at least the past week."

"Where are you living?"

"With her, on her ranch just north of Merkle."

"That's it then. No one had the guts to tail you out of town."

"Someone must of. Deaton knows."

Patrice's face fell. She sucked in a deep breath and let it out slow as she shook her head. "That's why you were racing out of the building? What did he say to you?"

"Before or after he fired me?"

The other woman did a double take. "He did what?"

"Shhhh!"

"Sorry." She lowered her voice. "Can he do that?"

"Not without board action but he's recommending to the board that I be let go. He's going to have them take it up at the next board meeting."

"When's that?" Patrice's face creased with lines the woman in her thirties didn't normally show.

Emmie shrugged and spread her hands. "After the Christmas break, in January, sometime."

"You need to talk to the union rep."

Scoffing, she nudged her own coffee away. "What's he going to do?" She leaned forward and whispered, "Bart Leeds is as homophobic as they come."

"He has to represent you Em. That's his job. You need the union behind you if this turns into a fight."

"Not him. You know how he got elected to the position?"

Patrice gave a half shrug. He was in there when I started here a few years ago."

Leeds is a typical Texas good old boy. He teaches primarily so he can coach the wrestling team and coach football. His whole goal in life is to become the head football coach. He was ramrodded through over a more qualified woman who ran against him."

"If you won't talk to him, at least talk to somebody. Call the state teacher's association if that's what it takes."

"Let's see what happens first. Frankly, if they let me go, so be it. I'll get by until I start at the college. I'm not destitute."

"It's not a matter of getting by, Em. It's about being fair; doing what's right by people. And, what about the kids? What happens to them if they let you go before the end of the year? A series of substitutes? It's hard to get somebody out here to sub as it is. You're talking about four or five months that your classroom door may be a revolving door."

"I hadn't thought about it like that."

CHAPTER 22

Thursday Evening, December 15th

"What's wrong?" Cass asked.

Emmie gave her a sidelong glance. She didn't even know where to begin. She opened her mouth to speak, but before the words could come, Jimmy tromped up on the porch and poked his head through the screen door.

"Gran's car is coming up the driveway," he announced. "Looks like she's driving."

"Oh," Cass said, "this can't be good."

They all went out to the porch. When Rosa Lute stopped her car behind Jimmy's pickup, Cass rushed to her and opened her door. "Gran, what's wrong? You know you're not supposed to be driving right now with your leg...your hip...everything. Are you hurt?"

Rosa waved her granddaughter off. "Everything is fine and I'm perfectly capable of driving a car three miles on back country roads. Been doing it since I was ten."

When she shifted around in the seat, Cass instinctively reached out to help her out of the car. Rosa slapped at her outstretched hand. "I got myself in here. I can get myself out."

As she ambled slowly to the porch with Cass trailing close behind, she called out to Emmie. "Hello there! It was you I came to see."

"Me?"

"Aren't you the chief party planner for this shindig we're going to have?"

"Umm, yes…yes ma'am."

"Well then, we have a lot of work to do and a week to get it done. I'll do the paperwork; you all do the leg work."

Emmie dipped her head in acknowledgment at the old woman.

While Jimmy pulled a disappearing act, Emmie turned and led the way into the house, smiling to herself. She started toward the living room, but Rosa had other ideas.

"Let's do this here in the kitchen. This isn't going to be chit chat. This is going to be serious planning."

"Yes ma'am," both women said, in unison.

"Cass, we're going to need some paper and pens."

The stocky brunette turned and strode toward her home office.

Emmie was nervous, being alone with Rosa. "Can I get you anything Mrs. Lute? A glass of tea? Some coffee?"

"You best start calling me Rosa…or even Gran, like those two do." She waved a hand about, indicating Cass and Jimmy.

"Okay…alright, Rosa." Em wasn't too sure she was ready to call her Gran just yet.

Rosa worked herself into the seat at the head of the table that Cass usually took. Emmie moved off to her usual side.

"I admit, I didn't care for the idea when Cass came over and first brought it up but, when it comes down to it, I've never been one to miss a good party. Since this is supposed to be at my place,

I want to make sure it's a good one; not something just slapped together."

Emmie wasn't sure if she should feel offended, but then admitted to herself that, since they'd first talked about it, they'd done little to plan it.

When Cass returned, she took Jimmy's usual spot across from Emmie without even a glance at her Grandmother. She passed out the paper and pens without a word, then looked at Rosa Lute expectantly.

Rosa started right in. "We are still in agreement that this will be at my ranch, right?"

The other two women nodded.

"So, what have you two accomplished since that time? Quite frankly, I see no evidence of any sort of party planning, from my perspective." She sat back in her chair and looked at each of them in turn.

Cass grimaced. "I've, uh told a few people. Pam knows. A few people at school. They all say they'll come. I've been kind of busy to do much else."

Rosa pointed a thin finger at Emmie. "And you?"

"I've invited my family, of course. A teacher I work with… that's about it. Nothing formal, I'm afraid."

"We need to get some real invitations out there right away. Tomorrow even. Let's start a guest list." She looked at Cass. "Take these names down. I'm going to leave it up to you to get the invites out."

"But, there's school and…"

Rosa held up a hand. "You want to have this party or not?"

"Yes ma'am."

"Then no excuses." She looked at Emmie, "You good with a computer?"

Em nodded.

"Good. I'm not and neither is she," she said, as she jerked a finger at Cass. "Print up something nice but simple that gives the date and time."

"For mailing?" Emmie asked.

The Lute matriarch shook her head. "There's no time for that. Much as I hate the thought, it's going to have to be some type of flier or some such thing."

She proceeded to throw a bunch of names at Cass for her to write down. When they were finished wracking their own brains, Rosa took the paper from her Granddaughter and slid it over to Emmie. "Add all your family and such on there. Everybody you can think of."

"Uh…okay." *Whoo boo! There's a rabbit hole I don't want to go down.* When she realized she was being watched, she started to add names to the list.

"We'll need a proper Christmas tree," she said to Cass. "You and Jimmy go out Saturday and cut down one of those Loblolly's your Pap planted."

Cass's eyes widened. "Are you sure you want to do that?"

"I don't say what I don't mean. You know that."

"They're growing fast Gram. Some of them are over twenty feet high."

"All the more reason to cut one down. We have 18 feet to work with in the great room, so keep that in mind. Besides, most of them will have to come down, when we put in the wind farm. Can't have them shielding the wind as they grow." She was on a roll. "Write this down somewhere else. Look into relocating the rest of those trees on or off my ranch. Donate 'em. Whatever we need to do."

Cass dutifully made a note.

"How are you coming with that list?" Rosa asked Emmie. She looked over the paper and scoffed, "Surely you know more people than that?"

"I was just thinking that it's so close to Christmas," Emmie began, "and people will already have plans…"

Rosa interrupted her. "I know what this is really about. First off, this time around, the party is at my house. You two can make your relationship known or you can try and keep it private. Eventually, people are going to figure it out. They'll come because they were invited. If they leave because they disapprove of the two of you, then that's their problem, not ours."

When you put it that way..." I'll print up something tonight and we can pass mine and some of yours out at the tailgate tomorrow in Arlington. Most of Sweetwater will be there." Emmie bent her head back to her task and started scribbling names on the list as fast as she could think of them.

"Now then," Rosa said, focusing back on Cass, "we need to talk about food. There will be brisket, of course."

"Of course," Cass and Emmie both echoed in response.

"We have to have that," Rosa continued. "That's tradition."

Em nodded. "In my family too. My mother might be annoyed if we upstage her Christmas Eve spread, however."

"Then upstage we shall," Rosa responded, raising an arm high.

Emmie couldn't help but laugh.

Cass didn't. She wasn't so sure it was a good idea. "It's not a competition Gran. Things are..." She eyed Emmie. "Let's just say her mother isn't taking her moving in here very well. For that matter, neither did you."

Rosa Lute nodded. "Fair enough. You're right, but I am coming around. This woman over here has been good for you." She glanced at Emmie and smiled. "Anyone can see that. Maybe we can help her mama see it too."

"Probably not by upstaging their Christmas Eve celebration."

"Okay, okay! We'll do it your way." She shook her head at Cass and then turned back to Emmie. "You tell us what else your mother makes, and we won't do a bit of that!"

They all laughed and got down to the business of planning the menu.

. . .

AN HOUR LATER, as Cass walked her Grandmother out to her car, Emmie sat back in her chair and listened to the sounds of Jimmy's footfalls as he paced the floor overhead. With the state championship on the line in less than 24 hours, she knew the teenager was a bundle of nervous energy. Cass was keeping him on a short leash for the evening. In the morning, he'd board a bus for Arlington. *A win tomorrow would make for one heck of a party all week.*

She let her mind wander then and thought back fondly to Christmas Eve's on the Oakes' ranch. It was always a big to do affair with her brothers and their families and her grandparents when they were alive. Food traditions were big in her family too. There was brisket, turkey and ham. Of course, with the brisket there were plenty of her mother's homemade pickles and onions one of the hands grew on a plot on the south range.

She and Seth usually stayed at the ranch on Christmas Eve, after the party, because Seth Senior stayed away from their home, in town, in Sweetwater, more than he was home after the first couple of years. He might come in for Christmas, he might phone it in. Those weren't good memories for her, but she did her best to make Christmas fun for Seth and to put on a good face in front of her family.

She did miss the little house they had in town. When they first married, she'd stepped away from the confines of the family. She enjoyed having her own place. She felt a little freer there, especially when Seth Senior was away. She moved back to the ranch after his death only for her son's sake. Though his father hadn't been around very much, he'd looked up to the man and looked forward to the times when he was home. Seth Sr. seemed to have a soft spot in his heart for his son, allowing him more time than he had Emmie in the last couple of years of his life. Young Seth started missing that immediately. At least at the ranch, he had another man he revered and looked up to in her father and her brothers were around often too, to let the boy just be a boy.

CHAPTER 23

Friday, December 16th

Emmie was glad she'd printed a stack of invitations. She and Seth met up with Cass, so she could pass a third to her. She kept the rest for herself. They split up again and worked the parking lot from opposite corners. She ran into several families she hadn't thought of when she was making her list the previous evening, and when she added to it as she sat in her nearly empty classroom for the half day session.

People were in high spirits, looking forward to the game. Their enthusiasm buoyed her own spirits as she walked along, stopping at each vehicle decorated in Mustang red and white. People took her hand, took an invitation and ruffled Seth's hair as he stood behind her at each stop, eying the spread of food that was invariably on display. By the time they'd turned the corner to work their second row, he'd already had a hot chocolate and three Christmas cookies.

Halfway down the row, a murmur rose in the lot. Em looked

around then pulled Seth in front of her and pointed. "Look, the marching band is forming up." They watched as the band director got his charges lined up and began to run them through their tune-up exercises. The thump of the drums and the blare of the horns added a little extra bounce to her step as she continued along on her mission.

When she arrived back at their own tailgate party, things were in full swing. Her mother looked her up and down. "You look a little winded. Where did the two of you get off too? No, never mind. Don't tell me. I'm sure she's here too."

"We was passing out…"

"Were, Seth," she corrected him. She looked at her mother and explained, "We were passing out invitations to the party next week."

Trudy Oakes leaned back and put a hand to her chest, striking a disapproving pose. "You're still going ahead with that?"

"We'll be there; don't you worry," Dusty said, as he stepped between the two women.

IT WAS quiet on the long ride back to Merkel. Jimmy rode shotgun beside Cass as she drove. He'd had to get permission from his coach to ride back with them instead of on the team bus. Now, he stared out the window, sullen.

Emmie sat in the back seat, tucked into the corner on the passenger side. Seth Jr. Slept, his head in his mother's lap. She knew Jimmie was thinking about the loss. There's no shame in being the state runner's up, she thought, but she kept her thoughts to herself. She figured Cass was probably thinking about all the chores that needed to be done, at first light.

It's been a long day. It will be a short night. Em tried to focus her mind on the party and everything that needed done for that, but she couldn't get the image of her mother's scorn out of her head. *No rest for the wicked.*

CHAPTER 24

Friday Evening, December 23rd

Rosa Lute directed traffic as Cass, Emmie, Jimmy and Cass's sister Pam ran about, doing her bidding. Pam's daughter Hailey, a 14-year-old, feminine version of Jimmy, entertained Seth Junior and kept him out of the way. The smell of smoked brisket, wafting through the outside air punctuated everything they did as they moved about the Lute ranch house and in and out. It was making Emmie hungry but there wasn't time to stop and eat.

"We've got less than an hour until folks start rolling in," Gran called out. "Let's start getting the food laid on."

They did as they were told, moving mountains of bread and rolls, a dozen jars of homemade pickles, and Cass's homemade barbecue sauces to the long row of serving tables.

Emmie shook her head, dazed. There was all the refrigerated food still to come, too. "There's way too much food, don't you think?" She looked between Cass and Gran.

Jimmy answered. "Nah. I'm so hungry, I'll eat a whole brisket by myself. A couple of my teammates said they'd come by too."

"There you go then," Gran said.

Emmie was skeptical. "Do you really think we'll have a lot of people here?"

Rosa started to tick off the names of everyone she knew was coming when they all heard gravel crunch in the driveway.

"That better be Aunt Alice," Cass said. "She promised to be here early to help set up."

"But we're almost done, right?" Jimmy asked.

Gran wagged a finger at him. "Not even close."

The knock on the door signified that it wasn't Alice. Cass looked out, then turned to Emmie. "Not someone I know. You?"

Emmie went to the door too. "It's Patrice, from school…the elementary school. She looks mad."

Emmie stepped out on the porch and greeted her friend.

Patrice waved her off. "I've been messaging and trying to call you for the last hour. The school board secretary's been trying to reach you too. When she couldn't, she called me and gave me a heads up."

"What? Why?"

The Superintendent called an 'emergency' closed door meeting of the school board. You probably have messages from Sue Ellen and from him. Lord knows, you've got a couple from me!"

Emmie beckoned Patrice to follow her into the house. She found her purse and dug out her phone. "We've been setting up for the party. I haven't checked this for hours." She saw multiple missed calls from Patrice and others from unfamiliar numbers. There were several texts from her friend, too.

"You're the guest of honor, so to speak, Em. It starts at 7:00. You need to get over there."

"There are voice mails." Emmie listened to one each from the secretary and the board President, Samuel Leto and two from Patrice. Leto advised her to call him back right away.

"You need to be here," Leto said moments later, when Emmie called him back. "This is just a hearing. We hope to keep it brief, so come alone. No need to bring a whole entourage with you."

"What about my union rep?"

He stifled a snort. "I hardly think that will be necessary. Again, this is just a hearing, at this stage."

You said that already, but I'm not convinced. "But I've got a family party starting in 45 minutes."

Sam Leto wasn't swayed. "We all have things we'd rather be doing tonight. If you value your standing with this school, you need to be here."

Cass looked on, concerning etching her features, as Emmie tried in vain to get in touch with the state representative she'd briefly spoken with after Patrice had recommended she do so a couple of weeks prior.

"No answer. Everyone has something better to do tonight than to be on call."

"What about your local rep?" Cass asked.

"No, no, no," Patrice responded, as she shook her head vigorously. "She's better off going it alone than taking him with her. They'll drum her out tonight and it won't even be a fair fight."

"They're going to drum me out anyway," Em said.

Cass looked over at her sister, who had been standing by silently, taking it all in. "Will you go with her?"

Pam nodded. "I'm not exactly up on school board policy and procedure but I can give them a run for their money; keep them honest."

Emmie shook her head, at that. "No, no. I know you have a

legal background but that isn't necessary. I don't want to put you out."

Pam raised an eyebrow and looked at Cass, "How much have you told her?"

"Um…we never really got that deep about you. She knows you work as a paralegal."

"Yes," Emmie said, "she's told me that. Am I missing something?"

Pam gave her a small smile. "I went to law school Emmie. I'm a licensed attorney and I keep my license current. I don't practice law for reasons that would take too long to explain right here, right now. We don't have the time. We need to get you to that so-called hearing."

"But what about the party…all this work?"

Cass pulled Emmie into a hug. "Go and knock 'em dead. The party will be here when you get back. I only wish I could go with you."

"Probably not the best idea," Pam said.

Patrice, standing by, forgotten in the flurry of calls and discussion, piped up; "I'm going. Let them try and stop me."

CHAPTER 25

When she was finally called in just after 7:20, Emmie rose but didn't move.

"Ready?" Pam asked her as she also stood.

Emmie smoothed her blouse and nodded.

"Just like we talked about on the way over here."

Emmie looked around for Patrice. The other woman had stepped outside to take a call several minutes before and hadn't reappeared. "Shouldn't we wait?"

The secretary beckoning to them again from the open doorway to the conference room, prompted Pam into motion. "Let's go. She'll catch up."

Pam led the way into the room.

Emmie peeked around the taller woman as all the men in the room stood. As she stepped to the forefront, she saw Samuel Leto frown through his oversize, wire-rim glasses. He waved a hand toward Pam.

"Who's this?"

Pam extended her hand to him. "Pamela J. Rogan. I'm Ms. Warren's lawyer and I'll be representing her at these proceedings."

Leto ignored her hand, pulled his glasses off and glared at Emmie. "There's no need for lawyers here. This is simply a…simply a…"

"A hearing?" Pam supplied.

"I uh…I wouldn't call it that!" He looked around helplessly at the rest of the board. No one returned his gaze.

From a row of chairs near the back of the room, Kenneth Deaton rose. "May I address the board?"

Leto gave him permission and resumed his own seat, but he left the two women standing.

Deaton looked first at Pam then focused on Emmie. "I…we…I guess I mean the board…there are some concerns and we…they wanted to address those."

"You are?" Pam asked Deaton.

"Dr. Deaton. He's the Principal at the elementary," Emmie answered for him.

"Very well," Pam began. "Dr. Deaton, let me ask you, is it the members of this board who have concerns involving my client, or is it just you?"

It was Kenneth Deaton's turn to look around the conference table at the men and women assembled there. Most returned his gaze, but no one spoke up. He walked toward the table and stopped just to the left of Wesley Trover. The two men looked at each other.

Emmie swallowed hard, trying to push back the acidic taste rising in her throat. Trover was only a generation removed from his bed sheet wearing, Klan ancestors. He kept getting elected because no one dared run against him. Emmie had always given him wide berth at official functions, just on principal. Now he had ammunition to come after her.

Trover broke the board silence. "Some things have come to our attention and we'd like to…uh…to hear from you, directly. Get the rumors out in the open and maybe even lay them to rest, little lady." He pointed at the chair they'd left empty at the end of the table. "Why don't you have a seat and we can talk like reasonable folks?"

Pam put out a hand to stay Emmie. "First of all, you'll address my client as 'Ms. Warren'. Second, I'll be doing all the talking. She'll answer only when I instruct her to answer." With that, Pam took a chair from the row Deaton had been sitting in and placed it next to the conference table chair. She indicated Emmie should take the new chair and she took the seat at the head of the table. She laid down a notepad and began to write the date and time at the top.

Leto found his voice. "There's no need to record any of what's said here tonight. It's all off the record."

Pam glanced at the board secretary who was noting every utterance and then addressed Leto, "We prefer to keep it all on the record."

Emmie couldn't contain herself. "If it's off the record, if nothing is official, why are we even here?"

Pam shot her a warning glance.

"No, let me say this. It's Christmas. I'm sure we all have other things to do. I know I do. We're here because whatever you had planned before I showed up with counsel, couldn't wait a couple of weeks. Someone," she tipped her head toward Deaton and Trover, "forced you all in here tonight, so let's hear why."

Before anyone could respond, a commotion of voices rose from outside the windows that ran down the east wall of the room. Leto tried to speak but the sounds of cow bells and raised voices drowned him out.

Sue Ellen got up from her seat on the east side of the table and moved the drapes enough to be able to peek out. "It's getting dark, so it's hard to see," she said, "but it looks like there are several people out in the parking lot."

Leto directed her over the din, "Go out there and tell them to take their little party elsewhere. We're trying to conduct serious board business in here."

Emmie gave Pam a knowing look and mouthed, "Patrice," to her.

OUTSIDE, the crowd was growing. The Merkel crew went into action after a text from Patrice, not five minutes after Pam's vehicle had left the driveway.

Cass called Cora and filled her in. She, in turn, rallied the rest of Emmie's family, most of whom were already preparing for the drive to Merkel, and had them detour over to the school board offices instead.

Neighbors started coming out of their homes on the usually quiet side street, to see what all the ruckus was.

A man recognized Cora's husband Fred and clapped him on the back. "Hey coach, great season!" he called out over the commotion. "To bad about the championship."

"Thanks," Fred managed. "The boys did great. Gave it their all." He trailed off, unsure what else to say.

Another man walked over to the two of them. "Hey coach! Great game! Too bad we lost, but we'll get 'em next year!"

"Thanks," Fred said. "Appreciate the support."

"So what's up here?" the second man called out. "Lotta racket!"

"Board's having an emergency meeting."

"Bout what?"

Fred spread his hands. "Long story. The gist is they're trying to drum my sister-in-law, Emmie Warren out now...tonight. She's uh...she's already resigned and she's leaving at the end of the year."

"Drum her out?" The first man asked. "Ms. Warren? My youngest boy had her a couple of years ago. He was always all gaga over her."

"Don't know her," the second man said, "but that don't seem right. Why would they do that in the middle of the year?"

Fred looked down and mumbled, "They think…they think she's gay."

"What's that you said?"

The doors opened and the board secretary, Sue Ellen Ryman stepped outside, waving her hands for calm. A hush went through the crowd as she walked into the lot.

A normally reserved woman, Sue Ellen rarely raised her voice. As the gathering crowd quieted, she announced, "There's been a special meeting of the school board called." She looked back over her shoulder at the boardroom windows. Light filtered through the curtains of two of them. She chose her next words carefully. "With your cooperation, we hope it will be a very short meeting." She winked at the people closest to her.

The crowd roared.

As Sue Ellen retreated back into the building, the second man addressed Fred again, "Did you say she's gay?"

When Fred didn't answer, he went on, "Why the hell would they have a meeting about that? That's not right."

Dusty Oakes heard part of the exchange between Fred and the other man. He didn't know the man, but his words loosened the tightness in his chest. He worked his way to the front of the crowd and, standing where Sue Ellen had stood moments before, whistled the crowd quiet. "I'm Dusty," he called out, "for those here that don't know me."

Laughter rang out.

He waved a hand to quell it. "What's going on in there isn't funny. This board is trying to railroad my daughter. I'm going to tell you what, it doesn't matter what they do. I support my daughter and the new love of her life no matter what. We were supposed to be having a party tonight to celebrate Christmas, to celebrate friends and family. I say we have that party right here!"

The crowd yelled back its approval. It was all the incentive

Rosa needed to start unloading the food and laying it out on tailgates around the little lot.

"WE'RE NOT GOING to get anywhere with this," Sue Ellen told the board from her vantage point by the windows. "They've brought in lights. Now neighbors are all coming out. Cars are pulling in. Someone put the word out."

The door opened, and Patrice walked in leading Barbara Shone and a few other teachers.

"This is a closed meeting," Leto said, as he jumped up and moved toward them.

"They're with us," Pam said.

Barbara smiled at Emmie. "And we're not leaving," she told Leto.

Wesley Trover looked between Deaton and Leto. "We need to do what we came here to do." He jerked a hand over his shoulder toward the windows. "Don't let them scare you."

"And don't let the voters scare you next election, Trover," Patrice said.

He smirked. "I'll be unopposed, as usual."

"Don't be too sure about that."

Leto went to the windows and opened a set of curtains a few feet. The light that poured out from inside stoked the energy of the crowd. When the people closest to the windows saw him, they rushed closer and taunted him. "Leave her alone Leto! Let her go!"

He pulled the drapes closed quickly and turned back to the other board members. "Forget it. It's a lost cause, no matter what we want to do. The tide is definitely against us tonight, and…it's Christmas."

. . .

As Samuel Leto conceded defeat, inside, a light dusting of snow started to fall outside. Dusty Oakes looked up and smiled, taking it as a sign. He smiled at Trudy, who had joined him at his side, right after his little speech. "It'll be gone before first light," he said, "but it sure is a pretty sight."

CHAPTER 26

Christmas Eve

"Last chance," Emmie said as she looked over at Cass. "Are you sure you want to do this?"

"I wouldn't miss it." Cass leaned over, bussed Emmie on the lips and then turned and got out of her truck. Emmie took a deep breath and joined her for the walk up to the house.

They walked into a melee of Oakes and Haines children. Seeing them, Seth ran to his mother and threw his little arms around her waist. "Mommy! I missed you today!"

"I missed you too, buddy," she said as she stooped to hug him. "I love you."

"I love you too." He backed away and grabbed for her hand. "I made you something. You have to see it!" He started to tug at her, but then stopped and looked at Cass. He reached for her hand too. "It's for both of you, for our tree. Come see!"

. . .

Emmie tucked Seth in then tiptoed back to the door. She closed it softly and smiled at Cass who stood waiting in the hallway.

"He's so tired, but he's so afraid he's going to miss something."

Cass grinned. "Sounds like things are settling down, downstairs too. Everyone is leaving."

The door to Seth's room creaked open and the boy peeked out.

"Seth Jr.!" Emmie waved a finger at him. "I thought you were asleep. Santa Claus can't come, if you don't go to bed."

"But mom...we didn't give you your present, yet."

"Yes, you did. That pretty sweater with the reindeer on it..."

"Not that mom. Tell her Cass!" He held out a wrapped box about the size of a candy box.

Emmie chuckled. "I suppose you want some of whatever's in there? Is that what this is about?"

Cass took the box from Seth and handed it to Emmie. "We were going to give you this tomorrow, but someone just couldn't wait." She reached over and ruffled the child's hair.

"Open it mommy!"

Emmie untied the ribbon made of twined crepe and carefully unsealed the wrapping paper as Seth shifted from foot to foot, impatiently. She lifted the lid off the box. Inside was a framed picture of Cass and Seth, her standing behind him, her hands on his little shoulders. They both had on hats and boots. Seth held a coil of rope in one hand and the lasso end in the other.

A tear formed in the corner of Emmie's eye. She looked up at Cass and shook her head. "When...when did you do this?"

"Grandma took it yesterday," Seth said.

"Rosa took this?" Emmie asked Cass.

"Not Gran Rosa, mommy. Grandma Trudy. It's for your desk at your new work." Cass simply nodded.

Emmie let her tears fall.

"Why are you crying? Don't you like it mommy?"

Emmie stooped to hug her son. "I love it. Now scoot. Back to bed!"

BACK AT HOME, Cass pulled a jewelry box out of the branches of their tree. "It's not a ring…not yet," she said.

"No. No. I…it's too soon."

Cass nodded as she opened the box to show Em the heart shaped locket inside. "It isn't too soon for me to tell you that I love you." She took the locked out of the box and let it dangle until the heart touched Emmie's hand and she took it from her.

"Does it open?"

"Of course," Cass said. She reached over and showed her. On one side was a picture of Seth from the chest up in his cowboy getup and on the other was Cass in hers, minus the hat this time.

Cass turned Emmie around and clasped the locket around her neck. "So, you'll always have the two of us with you, no matter what. I love you Em."

"I love you too."

"I knew I wanted to be with you the first time I saw you, standing at that lectern, calling out names." Cass said.

"No. You didn't. It didn't start then. I don't believe you."

"Let me show you, then," Cass said. She began kissing her lips, gently at first, but then deepening the pressure when Emmie melted against her.

ABOUT THE AUTHOR

Anne Hagan is a part-time employee and a full-time author. She and her wife live in a tiny town that's even smaller than the Morelville of her Mystery fiction novels and they wouldn't have it any other way. Anne's wife grew up there and has always considered it home. Though it's an ultra-conservative rural community, they're surrounded there by family, longtime friends and many other wonderful people with open hearts and minds. They enjoy spending time with Anne's son, with their nieces and nephews and doing many of the things you've read about in her books or that will be 'fictitiously' incorporated into future Morelville Mysteries and Cozies series books. If you've read about a hobby or a sport in either series, they probably enjoy doing it themselves or someone very close to them does.

Check Anne Out on her blog, on Facebook or on Twitter:

For the latest information about upcoming releases, other projects, sample chapters and everything personal, check out Anne's **blog** at https://AnneHaganAuthor.com/ or like Anne on **Facebook** at https://www.facebook.com/AuthorAnneHagan. You can also connect with Anne on **Twitter** @AuthorAnneHagan.

JOIN ANNE'S EMAIL LIST

Are you interested in **free books**? How about **free short stories**? For those and all the latest news on new releases, **opportunities to receive ARC copies, to Beta read** and more, please consider joining Anne's email list at: https://www.AnneHaganAuthor.com by filling in the pop up or using the brief form in the sidebar.

ANNE'S OTHER BOOKS

Anne is the author of the Morelville Mysteries mystery/romance series of books featuring Sheriff Melissa 'Mel' Crane and Special Agent Dana Rossi. She's also written the Morelville Cozies mystery series (a spin-off of the Morelville Mysteries featuring mothers Faye Crane and Chloe Rossi), and multiple romances featuring characters inside and outside of the world of Morelville.

Though most of her stories stand alone, Anne recommends that you read her books in the following order:

- Relic: The Morelville Mysteries - Book 1 (Free wherever eBooks are sold)
- Busy Bees: The Morelville Mysteries - Book 2
- Dana's Dilemma: The Morelville Mysteries - Book 3
- Hitched and Tied: The Morelville Mysteries - Book 4
- Viva Mama Rossi!: The Morelville Mysteries - Book 5
- The Passed Prop: The Morelville Cozies - Book 1
- A Crane Christmas: The Morelville Mysteries - Book 6
- Mad for Mel: The Morelville Mysteries - Book 7

- Broken Women (A standalone romance featuring two characters from the mystery series)
- Healing Embrace (The sequel to Broken Women)
- Hannah's Hope: The Morelville Mysteries - Book 8
- Opera House Ops: The Morelville Cozies - Book 2
- The Turkey Tussle: The Morelville Mysteries - Book 9
- Sullied Sally: The Morelville Mysteries - Book 10
- Finding Sheila: The Morelville Mysteries - Book 11
- Christmas Cakes and Kisses (A standalone romance featuring a character from the mystery series)
- Steamboat Reunion (The sequel to Healing Embrace)

- Loving Blue in Red States - Standalone short stories and collections of them
- A Sweetwater Christmas - A novella based on the Loving Blue in Red States short story, Sweetwater Texas

- Steel City Confidential – Anne's first legal thriller!

www.ingramcontent.com/pod-product-compliance
Lightning Source LLC
Chambersburg PA
CBHW072230190626
46809CB00017B/1676